Lucy Gordon cut her writing teeth on magazine journalism, interviewing many of the world's most interesting men, including Warren Beatty, Richard Chamberlain, Roger Moore, Sir Alec Guinness and Sir John Gielgud. She also camped out with lions in Africa, and had many other unusual experiences which have often provided the background for her books. She is married to a Venetian, whom she met while on holiday in Venice. They got engaged within two days. Two of her books have won the Romance Writers of America RITA® award.

You can visit her website at www.lucy-gordon.com

ITALIAN TYCOON, SECRET SON

BY
LUCY GORDON

MILLS & BOON®

Pure reading pleasure™

All the char‌   ‌tion
of the autho‌
same name ‌
individual k‌
pure inventi‌

All Rights ‌   or
in part in a‌   h
Harlequin E‌   r
any part the‌   n
or by any m‌   ng,
recording, s‌   e,
without the ‌

This book is sold subject to the condition that it shall not, by way of trade or otherwise, be lent, resold, hired out or otherwise circulated without the prior consent of the publisher in any form of binding or cover other than that in which it is published and without a similar condition including this condition being imposed on the subsequent purchaser.

® and TM are trademarks owned and used by the trademark owner and/or its licensee. Trademarks marked with ® are registered with the United Kingdom Patent Office and/or the Office for Harmonisation in the Internal Market and in other countries.

First published in Great Britain 2009
Harlequin Mills & Boon Limited,
Eton House, 18-24 Paradise Road, Richmond, Surrey TW9 1SR

© Lucy Gordon 2009

ISBN: 978 0 263 86940 8

Set in Times Roman 13 on 14½ pt
02-0509-47219

Printed and bound in Spain
by Litografía Rosés, S.A., Barcelona

CHAPTER ONE

ONE thing was clear from the start.

Mandy Jenkins and Renzo Ruffini were fated to be combatants: to tease, taunt and infuriate each other, to jeer and bang their heads against the wall in mutual exasperation. And then to laugh and forget everything. Until the next time.

The truth was there the night they met, if either of them had been able to see it: the instant attraction hiding behind antagonism, the meeting of minds that took them both by surprise.

The only thing missing was the tragedy. That came later.

It was an evening in late February when Mandy arrived in Chamonix, on the French-Italian border, and booked into one of the city's best hotels. It was slightly more than she could afford, but she was about to spend the next week living tough in the mountains and she reckoned she was entitled to spoil herself.

Everything was perfect, starting with the view from her bedroom window, of the mountains rearing up, shimmering white in the darkness, right down to the delicate French cuisine in the restaurant.

She took her time over the meal, occasionally glancing around at the other diners. One couple in particular claimed her attention. The woman was roughly in her late thirties, done up to the nines, evidently with the intention of attracting a conquest.

Laying it all out, Mandy mused.

If so, the woman was successful. The man with her was entirely focused on her ripe beauty, holding her hand, fixing his eyes on her as though the rest of the world didn't exist. He too seemed to be in his thirties, with a face that was attractive rather than handsome. But the attraction was intense. His features were lean and sharp, the eyes brilliant with intelligence and devilment.

He smiled, and it was beaming, dazzling, all enveloping.

Hmm! Mandy thought.

Many women would have been seduced by that smile, even at this distance. But not her. She'd seen something that didn't ring true. Despite his fervour, the passionate intensity in his gaze, this man wasn't in love. He was simply doing what was expected of him in the situation, heading down a well-worn road to a predetermined end. And there were no prizes for guessing what the end would be.

Her impression was confirmed a few minutes later when the couple rose and headed for the lift, his arm around her waist, her head on his shoulder, their gazes locked in mutual adoration.

After drinking her coffee, Mandy retired to her own room to prepare for the next day when she would join an expedition up the mountains, led by professional climber, Pierre Foule. She was looking forward to it, knowing herself to be physically well equipped with a strong, young body, slim and lithe. Her black hair was cut short in a neat crop.

Efficient, she thought. *Just what's needed.*

What she didn't take into account was her deep green eyes. To her they were just eyes, useful for their perfect vision, but not special, so she entirely missed their beauty and the effect they could have on other people.

The shower felt unbelievably good, and when she'd finished and put on a towel robe, she felt invigorated and ready for the climb she would start tomorrow.

The thought filled her with the desire for one

last look at the mountains, and she slipped out onto the wrought iron balcony to stand enraptured. She was about to go back inside when a commotion reached her from two windows along. A man was cursing in French, a woman was screaming.

The window was at an angle and she had a clear view as the curtains parted and a man rushed out onto the balcony.

It somehow came as no surprise to discover that he was the same man she'd been studying downstairs. Before her startled gaze, he climbed onto the wrought iron railings, took a deep breath and launched himself towards the balcony of the next window, landing easily.

But there his luck ran out. There was only darkness inside and his tapping on the window produced no response. The noise from the place he'd just left was growing louder and Mandy saw him eye her own balcony with intent.

He was mad, she thought. The leap he'd just made was across a corner angle and relatively easy, if you were into that kind of thing. But the balcony where he stood now was straight across from hers, a good six-foot jump and a forty-foot drop if he missed it.

'You're out of your mind,' she called.

'Can we talk about that later?'

Aghast, she retreated into her room, just peering out far enough to see the moment when he launched himself into space, clearing the gap with ease and only just having to cling on to the railings as he landed, muttering, *'Grazie dio!'* just loud enough for her to hear. Italian, then.

But she'd called to him in English and she had to admire the aplomb with which he switched back to her language.

'Let's go,' he said hastily, hustling her inside and closing the window firmly.

'What the—'

'Hush,' he said urgently. 'Don't make a sound.'

'Who are you giving orders to?' she demanded, drawing the edges of her robe together. 'Just who are you?'

'A man who's throwing himself on your mercy,' he said quickly. 'Don't be alarmed; I'm not going to hurt you. I just need a place to hide until he gives up the hunt.'

'He? Who's he?'

'The husband, of course,' he said, in a tone that implied inevitable consequences. 'I didn't know there was one. She swore she was divorced, and how's a man to know?'

'*She* being the woman you had dinner with downstairs, I suppose?'

'Oh, you saw her? Can you blame me for losing my head?'

'You didn't lose your head,' she said, standing back and regarding him cynically. 'You knew exactly what you were doing at every moment. All that passionate gazing—' She made a gormless face to indicate what she was saying and he flinched.

'That's a wicked slander! I never look like that.'

'Look? Present tense? Meaning not with her or any of the others?'

'How do you know there are others?'

'Guess! You looked like a lovesick duck!'

'A *duck*? May you be forgiven!'

'But there was nothing lovesick about you. You were in control all the time.'

'It seems like it, doesn't it? A man who was in control would hardly be on the run. She just made my head spin.'

'And that's your excuse for acting like the hero of a bad Hollywood movie? Who do you think you are? Douglas Fairbanks?'

'Who?'

'He was always doing that athletic stuff in his films and— *Why am I telling you this?* How dare you just barge in here like some second-rate Lothario?'

'I thought I was Douglas Fairbanks,' he said

with an expression of innocence that didn't fool her for a minute.

'Get out! *Get—*'

The last word was silenced by his hand over her mouth.

'Hush, for pity's sake,' he begged. *'Ow!'*

'Now will you let go of me?'

'You bit my hand.'

'I'll bite you somewhere a lot more painful if you don't leave my room. Go back to your lady friend.'

'I can't, her husband will kill me.'

'Good for him! I'll help him dispose of the body.'

'You're not very kind,' he protested plaintively.

She stared at him, bereft of speech long enough to hear a knock at her door.

'Mademoiselle, I am police. Please to open at once. This is for your own protection.'

She darted to the door, but at first she didn't open it. Afterwards she could never quite understand what had stopped her, but she merely called back, 'What is the matter?'

'A criminal, *mademoiselle*. He has been detected in a room along here but managed to escape. Please to open.'

'Open it,' her companion murmured in her ear.

'What?'

'If you don't, they'll just get more suspicious. Your best bet is an air of calm and lofty innocence.'

'How dare you? I *am* innocent!'

'Then you can open it.'

'And let them see you, so that the husband can identify you?'

'He can't. He never saw me. I got away while he was still in the outer room.'

'And how do I explain your presence?'

'This is a liberated age. You're entitled to have a man in your room.'

'Are you daring to suggest that I pretend that you and I—'

'Unless you can think of something more convincing. I suppose I could be trying to sell you insurance—'

'*Shut up!*'

'Whatever you say. I'm at your mercy.'

'*Mademoiselle!*' That was the policeman again.

Then another man's voice said, 'He's obviously in there. Beat the door down.'

There was a thump on the door. Furious with all of them, Mandy wrenched it open so fast that the attacker was caught in mid-blow, lunging forwards against her and landing hard enough to knock her back. Only the swift movement of her mysterious companion prevented her hitting the wall.

'Murderer!' he cried. 'My darling, has he hurt you?'

'I'm not sure,' she said faintly. 'Help me up.'

He did so, lifting her in his arms and carrying her towards the bed, laying her down, then sitting beside her, still holding her.

'Get out, the pair of you,' he said to the two other men who were just behind him. 'Look what you've done.'

Through half closed eyes Mandy surveyed the two men, one of whom was in a police uniform. Madness seized her and she pointed to the other intruder, a squashy-looking individual with a mean face.

'Why did he attack me?' she asked in a quavering voice.

'I didn't, I didn't,' he squeaked. 'I was seeking the man who was with my wife. I thought he was here—'

'Ooh!' she moaned, covering her face and turning so that the stranger's arms enfolded her.

'Get out before I have the law on you,' he threatened.

The policeman began a stumbling apology but fell silent when he saw a look in the stranger's eyes. A jerk of the head sent him retreating through the door, half dragging the outraged husband with him.

'It's all right, they've gone.'

Lifting her head, she saw him regarding her with a mischievous devil in his eyes. Then her appalled glance fell on herself, and the towel robe which had drifted open, revealing her nakedness. Sanity descended on her like a cold shower and she snatched the edges together.

'Thank you for everything you did,' he said in a placating voice. 'You were wonderful.'

But he backed away as he spoke, reading murder in her eyes.

'If,' she said, breathing hard, 'you don't get out of this room this instant, I shall scream the place down, call back the policeman and tell everyone the truth about you.'

'Not that,' he begged. 'Anything but the truth.'

'Oh, but this truth is very interesting. You are an unspeakable scoundrel—'

'No doubt about it.'

'A crook—'

'Guilty.'

'A ham actor—'

'That's going too far.'

'A fraud, a man without scruple—'

He'd reached the door now, opened it, paused in the gap.

'I just want to say that you were brilliant,' he said quickly.

'Go!'

'And thank you.'

'If you don't get out of here—'

He paused just long enough to blow her a kiss. Then he was gone.

Mandy stood, torn between exasperation and laughter. He was everything she'd called him and worse, but she felt mysteriously invigorated as never before in her life.

Swiftly she put out the lights, tossed aside the robe and jumped into bed, mulling him over.

Where did he come from? She'd heard him mutter to himself in Italian, and he spoke in a Continental accent.

What had possessed him to make those crazy jumps? Fear of an enraged husband? No way. He was a lithe and powerful athlete who could have handled any number of husbands. Yet he'd chosen to run for it, risking his life in the process.

A man without fear, then, but also a man with some very kooky values. The way he'd said, 'She swore she was divorced, and how's a man to know?' implied many other similar incidents.

And it didn't bother him. It was just how he lived, from one woman to the next. He loved, he escaped, he went on. And he laughed. He'd been laughing all the time she'd berated him, not outwardly but inside. It had been there in his whole attitude, but mostly in his gleaming eyes.

Curse him for seeing her robe fall open. Just let him dare get ideas about her. She didn't have a husband, but she did have a very useful left hook.

The thought made her feel better, and she fell asleep.

Next morning Mandy set out to walk the short distance through the snow-lined streets of Chamonix that led to the office where she was to join the expedition. Up ahead loomed the dazzling white mountains, inviting her to forget everything earthbound.

As she reached the office of Pierre Foule, expedition organiser, she could see a group of young people outside, looking around and up, impatient for the pleasure to begin.

'When I told them at work that I was going to be climbing the Alps,' a man was saying, 'they were really impressed. Especially the girls.'

'And aren't you just going to make the most of it when you get back!' another man ribbed him.

From behind Mandy a young female voice joined in the banter. 'You want to be careful.

These days we climb them ourselves, and we get to the top before you.'

There was a good-natured laugh. Mandy turned to see a woman of about her own age, with a cheerful face and a robust appearance.

'Hi, I'm Joan Hunter,' she said. 'I'm going on the Mont Blanc trip.'

'Me too. I'm Mandy Jenkins.'

They looked each other over approvingly.

'I've just been in there to register,' Joan said. 'But it's a madhouse. Pierre Foule, who was supposed to be leading us, is off sick, so someone else is standing in, and the girls are crowding round him, sighing. Not that he's fending them off.'

'Oh, heavens!' Mandy said cynically. 'One of *them*.'

'Them?'

'All easy charm and full of himself.'

As soon as they went inside she saw what Joan had meant. A female crowd was converging around a man she couldn't see clearly. Then he turned and her blood froze.

'It can't be,' she whispered.

But there was no mistaking that smile, that air of being on top of life and ready for anything. She breathed hard.

'Hello, everyone,' he said. 'I'm Renzo

Ruffini. I'm taking charge of this trip, but I'm still missing someone.' His voice faded as Mandy appeared before him.

She had the pleasure of seeing him disconcerted, which she guessed didn't happen very often.

'You,' he whispered.

'Yes, me. I'm glad you remember me among the crowd.'

'But of course I do. You saved my life.'

'I think the least said about that the better, don't you?'

'Definitely.' He pulled himself together. 'How do you come to be here?'

'I'm Mandy Jenkins.'

'*You?*' he queried. 'Are you sure?'

'Well, I've been Mandy Jenkins for twenty-seven years. If there was a mistake, I'm sure I'd have noticed by now.'

'I only meant—you're not quite what I expected.' He surveyed her five foot two inches. 'It's a very demanding climb. I wonder if you're strong enough.'

'I've filled in the forms, answered all the health questions. I meet your requirements, otherwise I wouldn't have been accepted by Pierre Foule.'

'That's true, but if Pierre had realized you were quite so delicate—'

'Oi!' she said. 'Delicate, my left foot! I'm as tough as old boots.'

To prove it, she adopted a boxing stance, which he immediately copied, declaring, 'Put 'em up.' Then he ruined the effect by asking, 'That is what they say, isn't it?'

'That's what they say when they're going to thump someone. I'll thump you.'

'No, no, *ti prego, ti prego*,' he said in a comically placating tone. 'You may not be delicate but I am.'

'Will you please stop your nonsense?'

'Anything you say,' he vowed, giving her a delightful smile.

It was so obvious that this came from the manual of 'how to deal with awkward customers' that she nearly did thump him.

'Look,' she said in a low voice, 'I don't like this any more than you do, but we're stuck with each other. I joined to go up the Alps, and that's what I'm going to do.' She glowered in what she hoped was a threatening manner, not easy as he was ten inches taller. 'Do you understand?'

'*Signorina,*' he said solemnly, 'I vow to you that if I was an Alp I'd be shaking in my shoes.'

'Perhaps you should be,' she warned him.

Then he murmured something in Italian, clearly not expecting her to understand. But she did. He'd said, 'Why does this kind of thing always happen to me?'

She answered him in Italian. 'Some people act like a magnet for trouble.'

She had the reward of seeing him embarrassed.

'I shall have to beware of you, shan't I?' he said wryly.

'Definitely. You have been warned.'

'If you'll excuse me, I must speak to the others.'

Renzo moved away hastily.

'Cheeky devil,' she murmured. 'So certain that he's got everything sussed. And I bet they all fall for it. Well, not me.'

Mandy had to admit that the charge of 'delicate' had some truth. She was daintily built and graceful of movement, which fooled many people into thinking her fragile. They were wrong.

Joan returned to her side, saying, 'They say he's in great demand.'

'Because of his mountaineering skills, you mean?' Mandy asked ironically.

'I think it has more to with the *Wow!* factor,' Joan mused, studying Renzo's tall, athletic figure.

'I can't say I noticed it.'

Joan chuckled. 'You would have done if you weren't miffed with him.'

Mandy laughed and conceded the point. While she might not have taken to Renzo, honesty forced her to admit that he had the *Wow!* factor in spades.

If asked to describe his attractions, she would have shrugged and said, *Par for the course,* which would have been true without doing him complete justice.

He looked like a vibrant, healthy animal who'd spent his life in the open. Without being muscle-bound, he was powerful enough for the demands he obviously made on his lithe body. Even his dark hair and eyes fitted her picture of the conventional Italian male.

'A professional Lothario,' she said cynically, remembering the night before.

'So who's complaining?' Joan asked. 'I'm not.'

'He's all yours.'

At last the formalities were finished and Renzo called for their attention so that he could outline the plan for the next few days.

'We'll spend the nights in the huts we'll find up there,' he said. 'Some are like good hotels, some are more basic, but I take it you're all ready to rough it.'

There was a murmur of agreement and Mandy couldn't resist calling, 'Even those of us who are delicate.'

Renzo grinned. 'I guess I'm not going to be allowed to forget that. Right, let's go.'

As the others made their way out of the door, he drew her aside, murmuring, 'I really am grateful. You're not mad at me, are you?'

'I can't think what you're talking about. I remember nothing.'

'You're probably right. Let's be off.'

The first day was relatively easy, moving slowly up the lower slopes, linked by ropes.

Mandy had done just enough climbing to be able to cope fairly easily. The hardest moment was when Joan, roped to her, missed her footing. Briefly Mandy found herself supporting the young woman's weight, and hung on grimly, but Joan recovered quickly and the moment passed. Looking up, she found Renzo watching her and had the satisfaction of seeing him nod in a way that suggested she'd done well.

There was also the ironic pleasure of discovering that she was far from being the worst of the party of twelve. That honour was reserved for Henry, a hulking, loutish young man. Though superficially good-natured, he wanted to do everything his own way and didn't take kindly to instructions. Several times Renzo had to be very firm with him, and

Mandy had to admit that he managed it without trouble.

As the light faded they came to the hut where they would spend the first night. It was small and when they had all crowded in the place was bursting at the seams, but the food was filling, the beds narrow but adequate and there was an air of jollity that carried them through the evening.

It amused her to see that as soon as they arrived Renzo became the target of attention again. The women gazed at him with pleasure, the men with jealousy. He accepted it all as his due, and Mandy had to admit that he had plenty of what the Italians called *bella figura*. More than mere good looks, it implied confidence, style, charisma, panache.

He was never at a loss. When someone produced a battered guitar he led the singalong with all the aplomb of a natural showman.

Now and then Henry butted in, making a noise—as someone observed—like a terrified monkey. But he was shouted down and vanished, scowling. After that nobody thought of him until bed time, when the sound of a slap followed by a yell showed that he'd had no luck there, either.

The next day they climbed up nearly three thousand metres and ended in a larger hut, perched on the edge of a ridge, staring down into the valley where the lights of Chamonix were just visible, like winking signals from another planet.

Mandy slipped outside to catch the last of the light, which had an unearthly quality here, in the heart of the snowy peaks. In the distant sky she could see a blaze of glorious scarlet, such as she'd never expected in February, and held her breath, longing for it to last.

A door behind her opened and she glanced back to see Renzo emerge. To her relief, he didn't speak but stood in silence while they both watched the blazing colour fade swiftly into darkness.

At last she heard him sigh.

'It's breathtaking, isn't it? I always come out to watch.'

'And yet you must have seen it so often,' she ventured.

'It doesn't matter how often. It's always like the first time.' He looked at her wryly. 'I guess that surprises you, seeing as you have me down as an unrelieved jerk, totally insensitive and incapable of appreciating a moment of beauty. Don't deny that that's your opinion of me.'

'I wasn't going to deny it—' she chuckled '—why should I?'

He looked aggrieved. 'It might have been polite.'

'I don't do polite.'

'Very wise. You save a lot of time that way.' He came and sat beside her. 'Are you coping all right?'

'I'm fine, thanks. I'm really pleased with myself for not collapsing when Joan lost her footing. I just supported her until she was ready, you have to admit that.'

'True, but with me above, supporting the two of you. All right, all right, don't eat me.'

From inside came a burst of laughter, making him wince.

'Shouldn't you be getting back to your guests?' she asked.

'They're not my guests, they're my responsibility, and sometimes it's one I'd much rather do without. I swear, this is the last time I take over a party where I haven't been able to vet everyone first. And no, I don't mean you.'

'I know,' she said cheerfully. 'Henry. Do you know which one of the girls slapped him last night?'

He grinned. 'They're lining up to lay claim. Poor Henry. I saw him trying to attach himself to you earlier today. Is he giving you trouble?'

She glared. 'You're not chivalrously offering to take care of him for me, *I hope*.'

'No way,' Renzo said hastily. 'You deal with

him any way you like, and er—' he gave her a significant glance '—I'll dispose of the body.'

'All right,' she said, laughing. 'Enough said. Actually, Henry really wanted to have a moan about you.'

'Because I had to keep him in line?'

'I think it's more that you're everything he wants to be and never will. He reckons you don't get your face slapped, and that makes him want to kill you.'

'What does he think I'm up to? Those bunk beds are only about two feet wide.'

'Well,' Mandy mused, 'I suppose two feet might just be enough if—' She left the implication hanging.

'You're making me blush, do you know that?'

'I should really like to know what could make you blush,' she said ironically. 'Nothing I could think of.'

It was too dark for her to see much of his face, but his eyes seemed to gleam at her with unholy glee.

'How do you know if you don't try?' he teased.

'Now, you stop that,' she said, suddenly cross. 'I know what you're doing and it's a waste of time.'

'Sure about that?'

'Quite sure. Who do you think you're dealing

with? One of those girls in there, ready to sigh every time you go past?'

'I've never pictured you like that,' he said truthfully.

'You think I want you swinging from *my* balcony?'

'No way. You'd push me off.'

'How astute of you.'

'Let's drop this, since I'm getting the worst of it. I think I'll get us something to drink so that we can fight in comfort.'

Renzo went inside and Mandy leaned back in her chair, feeling content. She had a feeling of being in control, and she suspected that not many women had ever felt that with this man. It was very enjoyable.

CHAPTER TWO

RENZO returned after a moment with a bottle of light wine and two glasses.

'Just a little,' he said. 'We'll need all our wits about us tomorrow.'

When he'd poured and handed her the glass he said, 'So Henry behaved himself?'

'Only at first,' Mandy replied. 'Then he tried it on, but I gave him my "drop dead" look. It worked a treat.'

'He has all my sympathy. You're probably a karate instructor in your spare time.'

'No such luck. I do research.'

'Research? You mean—brainy stuff?' He sounded nervous.

'Well, I do have a couple of degrees.'

'A *couple*?' He edged away, as though fearful that her degrees would jump out and attack him.

'It helps. I hire myself out to people writing

books. They need stuff on other countries, history, language, that sort of thing.'

'Is that how you come to speak Italian?'

'That's right. I had to learn some for a man who was writing a novel about the Borgia family and all their evil doings, and I liked it so much I went on and learned the rest.'

'And I'll bet that's not the only language you know,' he said, sounding more cautious by the minute.

'I did French and German at school. They're often useful too.'

'You really are an academic.' He sounded aghast.

'Sure I am. Why do you keep looking down at the drop?'

'I was wondering which would be the best place to throw myself off,' he said in a hollow voice.

'Don't be in such a rush. Wait until we're all safe, and I'll think of something.'

They grinned in perfect understanding, and he refilled her glass.

'You're probably winding me up,' Mandy said, sipping appreciatively. 'I expect you went to college too.'

'For a couple of years, but I was there on an athletic scholarship. As long as I won things, my lack of brains didn't matter too much.'

She didn't believe a word of it.

'Don't you ever want to write books?' he asked.

'I've done a couple of travel books.'

'Is that why you've got a notebook?' he asked, observing something in her hand. 'You're actually working out here?'

'Just making a few notes. I do it wherever I am.'

'Don't you ever stop and simply enjoy yourself?'

'But I do enjoy myself when I'm jotting things down. Often I only know afterwards how I'm going to use them. They dance around in my head and take on a life of their own, and who knows what may come of it?'

'Fantastic,' he agreed at once. 'Throw the dice in the air and watch to see what happens.'

'I guess that's how you live.'

'I like to let life surprise me, just like you. We're alike, plenty of freedom and no ties. That's the way to be.'

'How do you know I have no ties?'

He shrugged. 'You're either free or you have a partner who's content to sit at home while you climb mountains.'

A little devil prompted her to say primly,

'And why not? We each follow our own path out of mutual respect.'

Renzo's face was a picture of comical disgust. '*Dio mio!* You ought to get rid of him fast. Hell would freeze over before I let my woman risk her neck without me there.'

'Let? *Let?* What century are you living in?'

'Any century rather than one where this can happen. But you're fooling me, aren't you? Don't tell me this paragon of dreary virtue actually exists.'

'No, he doesn't.' Mandy gave a melodramatic sigh. 'I just dream of meeting him.'

'Sure you do. And it would serve you right if he turned out to be just like you described.'

'What about you? No ties and you mean to keep it that way?'

'For a while at any rate. Ties are all right— one day.'

'No, I think you'll live and die a free man, because that's what life means to you.'

He raised his glass in salute. 'Very clever of you.'

She lifted hers in response. 'So be careful what you say. I see everything. I'm a witch.'

He peered at her in the shadows.

'No,' Renzo said softly, 'not a witch, a cat— a sleek, graceful, green-eyed cat.'

'Then beware my claws,' she said, suppressing the flare of pleasure that this gave her.

'I'll take my chances, because it's so nice to talk to someone who understands freedom. But, at the risk of being bopped, I'd like to know why you're alone. Have the men no eyes?'

'Perhaps they don't always like what they see,' she mused. 'He said he preferred a woman with "a bit of meat on her".'

Renzo nodded, far too intelligent to ask who 'he' was.

'He sounds like an Englishman,' he observed. 'That's the charming way they talk. But you speak of him in the past.'

'One day he just didn't turn up for a date and I never heard from him again.'

'You're well rid, and it saves you the chore of dumping him.'

'How do you know I would have dumped him?'

He made a face. 'Because you have too much taste to tolerate for long a creature who has the soul of a pig. And, besides, you'll never find your perfect man, because you're not really seeking him.'

Mandy thought for a moment. Could that possibly be true? The man who'd almost broken her heart—but only almost—wasn't she recovering remarkably fast?

She had a strange sensation that Renzo had looked directly into her and seen things that were hidden from herself.

'That might be it,' she conceded, nodding slowly.

'What made you come up here? It's more than seeking material for your notebooks.'

'I needed the change. I like to get out in the open and do something adventurous. Slaving over a hot computer isn't enough.'

'I know. I spend too much time cooped up, as well.'

'I thought you'd practically live in the mountains.'

'I don't do this for a living. I used to climb a lot but now I sell sports equipment. I learned to climb with Pierre, who owns this firm, and is the man you were expecting. We've stayed friends, and when he needs help he calls me. It gives me the chance to get back here.'

'Away from noise and silly irritations,' she murmured.

Renzo nodded. 'The mountains may endanger you, but they're never trivial.'

'And even the danger—' She stopped and drew in a breath of pure satisfaction.

'You too? Yes, it's true. There's pleasure in going to the edge—perhaps closer than you should—'

'The moment when you feel you might just have gone too far,' she murmured, 'but you get away with it.'

'There's nothing like it,' he agreed appreciatively. 'And then you're a winner, ruler of the world. And next time—'

He stopped and their eyes met.

'Should you be talking to me like this?' she asked humorously. 'You—teacher. Me—pupil. Surely you should be preaching safety, not leading me astray with the delights of danger?'

'You're already "astray" or you wouldn't have known what I meant so quickly,' he said. 'But you're right. I shouldn't talk like that, and I wouldn't to anyone else. I rely on you not to repeat it.'

'I promise,' she said and they chinked glasses.

'Especially *him*!' Renzo added as Henry's bellow reached them from inside. It was clear that he was heading towards them.

'Is that the time?' Mandy asked hastily, rising. 'I think I'll get an early night.'

She was annoyed with Henry, who'd ruined a moment she was enjoying. The discovery that Renzo had hidden depths had opened a new path that might have been fun to explore. Best of all had been the understanding that had flashed between them. He was the last man with whom she would have expected this, which only made it more intriguing.

But she remembered that they would only be together for a few days. Then he would return to his country and she to hers, and that would be that.

Next day the weather was good and they travelled fast. With every step the air became clearer and brighter, and the peaks seemed tantalizingly closer.

'It's like we could get to the top today,' Mandy breathed when they were halfway up.

'That nearness is an illusion,' Renzo said. 'You've been in the mountains before, you should know all about the illusions.'

'True,' she said. 'So many different ones—'

'Yes, and after a while everything seems unreal—or maybe it's real—but how can you know when your surroundings seem to come and go? Are they near or far? What will it be like finding out? Or will we ever be able to find out at all?'

'Hey, you're a poet,' she said, grudgingly impressed.

'Nonsense,' he said hastily. 'I'm a serious-minded man, who disapproves of levity. And stop looking at me like that, you little cat. Sometimes I have to be serious—'

'Or pretend to be.'

'Or pre— Will you shut up, please? Listen to what I say, and be careful about false impressions.'

'But maybe not all the impressions are false.'

'Most of them out here *are*. Don't get sentimental, just concentrate.'

'Yes, *sir*!' Mandy gave an exaggerated salute.

'Behave yourself!'

This time she didn't answer in words, but her eyes said everything. He turned away quickly, yelling, *'All right everyone, are we ready?'*

Renzo went round the others, checking ropes, and Mandy gave a small, private smile. Without meaning to, she'd touched on a side of him that he preferred to keep private. Interesting. Very, very interesting.

They went further that day and finished up in a 'hut' that was an improvement on the last. Instead of dormitories with bunks, there were double rooms with comfortable beds. The food was excellent, and after a rewarding meal everyone gathered in the main room where a man was playing an accordion.

At first the dancing was boisterous, but after

a while the tone softened and the crowd divided into couples. Joan, Mandy was amused to notice, had two suitors to chose from—three, if you included Henry, which nobody did.

Joan's choice finally fell on a handsome young man called Peter. They circled the floor smoochily, then vanished together and weren't seen again.

Renzo danced with every girl on his expedition, except Mandy, who was so occupied he couldn't get near her.

What she hadn't told Renzo the night before was that she'd once wanted to be a dancer and had taken lessons. She'd given it up when she'd realized she had only a modest talent, but she still loved to dance, and suddenly the legacy of her training had kicked in. She could manage the fastest speeds, the most intricate steps, and men were soon queuing up to partner her.

One, a Frenchman called Marcel, was her equal. Together they hurled themselves about the floor, twisting, writhing, together and apart, while the others stopped dancing to stand back and watch.

They were Spanish dancers, clicking imaginary castanets, gazing passionately into each other's eyes. Then the rhythm changed, became rock 'n' roll, and he began to fling her up and around his shoulders. When the music crashed to a finish, she was lying back in his arms in a theatrical simulation of abandon. The applause was loud.

Marcel gave her a neat bow and set about turning his advantage to gold with the ladies who were converging on him. Slightly breathless, she smiled at her next partner, approaching her with his hands outstretched. But he was eased determinedly out of the way by Renzo.

'Boss's privilege,' he said. 'Mandy, I can't compete with your last partner, but I'll do my best.'

'Suppose I don't want to dance with you?'

'Doesn't matter,' he said with mock gravity. 'I have to distribute my favours equally. You're the only one left, and I can't have you being a wallflower, can I?'

'Wallflower? Me?'

But his eyes were gleaming with fun, and she thumped his shoulder lightly.

'Cheeky so-and-so,' she said. 'I don't know why anyone puts up with you.'

'I'm irresistible, hadn't you heard?'

'No, and if I do hear, I'll tell them different.'

'That's my girl.'

Renzo drew her close, sighing dramatically

in a way that made her want to giggle. The music had become a waltz, and as he guided her smoochily around the floor she realized that she was being stared at again, this time with envy.

'There's no need to overdo it,' she murmured.

'You don't understand. I'm *expected* to overdo it.'

'Ah, yes, just doing your duty. Otherwise, of course, nothing would make you dance with me.'

'I wouldn't go quite that far. A very large sum of money might persuade me.'

'I'll kick your shins in a minute.'

He was an excellent dancer and she fell easily into step with him.

'You're not playing your part,' he said after a while. 'You should be gazing adoringly into my eyes.'

Glancing up, she found his face closer than she'd expected and drew a sudden sharp breath.

'That's better,' he murmured.

'Watch it,' she murmured back. 'I'm in a dangerous mood.'

'Wonderful! A woman is never so interesting as when she's dangerous.'

Mandy knew a brief flare of alarm. For a moment—just for the tiniest possible moment—she'd actually wanted him to find her interesting. Time to bring him down a peg.

'That's a very good line,' she said admiringly. 'You must be proud of it.'

'One of my best,' he assured her.

'Of course you need to practise your delivery.'

'I thought I delivered it just right,' he said, hurt.

'No, you should try it with a woman who isn't standing back and judging the performance.'

'You're not standing back,' he said, tightening his arm about her waist, so that she could feel his body more closely against hers.

'*Inside* I'm standing back, having a good laugh at you, actually daring to think I'd give you an easy time.'

'If there's one thought that never crossed my mind it's that you'd give me an easy time,' he said fervently.

'Well, you should be able to cope with that,' she teased. 'You're Italian, after all. Think Casanova! Think Romeo!'

'Think a sock on the jaw! *Mio dio*, where do you get these ideas from? If I labelled you cold and prissy because you're English, you'd be annoyed.'

'Not if it were true,' she said. 'Then I'd be flattered that you'd recognised my innate virtue.'

His alarmed expression was so comical that she burst out laughing.

'I'd take a bet,' Mandy said, 'that every night

at bedtime you say a prayer to be saved from women of virtue.'

Renzo gave her a considering look. 'Well—maybe not all of them. How sad that the music is ending. We must continue this so interesting conversation another time.'

He gave her a little bow as they parted.

'Thank you, kind lady,' he said formally.

'And you, sir. With your duty done, you can start enjoying yourself.'

His eyes flashed her a message, but so swiftly that she wasn't sure she'd read it right. Perhaps it was safer that way.

Needing some fresh air, she fetched her jacket and slipped out into the snow. There was a full moon, bathing the mountains in dazzling silver light, and she walked down to the low wall that marked the boundary, where she could sit and ponder.

'Ah, there you are,' came a voice behind her.

She gave a silent groan. 'Hello, Henry.'

'I was watching you in there. You were fantastic.'

'Thank you.'

Inwardly she was praying that he wouldn't come and sit beside her. He did.

'You're such a super mover,' he enthused,

'slinky and sexy. It made me think all sorts of things about you and me. How about it, eh?'

'No,' she said firmly.

He made the mistake of lunging for her, which gave Mandy the chance to seize his hand in an iron grip.

'Ow!' he muttered.

'Listen carefully, Henry,' she said with a deadly smile. 'If you don't back off, I shall boil you in oil and decapitate you, not necessarily in that order. Now push off before I'm tempted.'

Even he got that message. He sloped off in the direction of the door, muttering just loud enough for her to pick up the word *frigid*. Furiously she picked up a handful of snow and hurled it after him.

'Hey!' protested a voice.

'How long have you been there?' she demanded indignantly.

'Long enough to enjoy the sight of Henry being an idiot,' Renzo said, coming forward, brushing snow off himself.

'Shouldn't you have rushed to my rescue? How about protecting a damsel in distress?'

'I never saw a damsel less in need of help,' Renzo said, sitting beside her. 'It's enough to make a man go very carefully.'

'If it was in his nature to go carefully. Some men don't have the common sense to be afraid.'

Renzo nodded. 'Except when I'm climbing, I never had any common sense,' he confirmed. 'It's led to me having my face slapped a few times, but it's also given me some of the best moments of my life.'

She nodded. It was just as she'd supposed.

'You were pretty gorgeous in that dance,' he said at last. 'Enough to make a man enjoy a few fantasies.'

'Only a twerp like Henry,' she said firmly.

But Renzo shook his head. 'Any man,' he said softly.

'Is this you doing your duty again?' she asked, regarding him cynically.

'Let's just say that if I wanted to approach you, I wouldn't go about it like a bull at a gate.'

It was madness to say, 'Just how would you go about it?' but she found herself saying it anyway.

'I'd be quiet for a moment while we both drank in the mountains. Then I'd point out how the moonlight makes them unearthly, so that we almost could be on another planet—just the two of us.'

'And then you'd say that there was nobody

you'd rather have with you than me?' she conjectured.

'I think I'd try something more subtle like—you're so ethereal that you seem to embody the moon. No?'

He'd seen the scepticism in her face.

'I might laugh at that one,' she admitted.

'Then how about something more down-to-earth like—watching you dance gave me thoughts I'm ashamed of. I couldn't even tell you about them—unless you insisted.'

'I don't think I need to,' she murmured.

'Of course not. You had a dozen men at your feet, as you well knew.'

'Did I?' she mused. 'Well, perhaps.'

'Little cat,' he whispered. 'You knew exactly what you were doing.'

Renzo was right. There had been pleasure in knowing that every man's eyes were upon her, but the only ones she'd cared about were his.

But hell would freeze over before she gave him an easy victory.

'One must pass the time somehow,' Mandy said languidly.

'Very good,' he said. 'Play the indifferent card. Make him suffer, but beware of teasing him too much, lest things get out of your control.'

'Nothing ever gets out of my control,' she mused softly. 'I don't allow it to happen.'

'Now that is sheer provocation.'

Somehow he'd taken possession of her hand and was holding it gently between his.

'Of course,' he said thoughtfully, 'this might be the moment when you threaten to pour boiling oil over me.'

'No, I think I'll save that until later.'

Without speaking, he laid his cheek against her palm. It was a pleasant sensation, and not alarming, until he turned his head so that she felt his lips. She controlled her tremor, determined not to let him feel it, but she couldn't hide it from herself. This was only meant to be a joke, but what had she wandered into?

'On the other hand,' she said softly, 'I know just the oil to use.'

'You think I'd be foolish to try my luck any further?'

'Very foolish.'

Renzo leaned forwards so that his mouth was close to hers. 'A brave man would put that to the test.'

'How brave are you?'

'Shaking in my shoes.'

The next step was so easy. She had only to say the word and she would be in his arms, his mouth on hers, relishing the kiss for which he'd been cleverly preparing her.

Preparing her!

Mandy froze as knowledge hit her like lightning.

It was a game, a trick, and she'd walked into it with her eyes open. He'd probably taken a bet with himself that he could lure her into dropping her defences. And she'd fallen for it. Nearly.

'Shaking in your shoes, hmm?' she mused. 'Well, I think that's a very good idea. If you knew what I was thinking right now, you'd really shiver.'

'Mandy—'

'Don't treat me like a fool, Renzo. I know what you're up to, and I'm ahead of you. You did it well, I admit, but not quite well enough.'

'You think I'm—'

'Just fooling. Admit it.'

'Well—' he seemed to consider '—since you saw through me so easily, I guess that's it. I might as well give up.'

'You and Henry both,' she said firmly.

After that there was nothing to do but walk casually back indoors, bid a cheerful goodnight to everyone, go to bed, and lie staring into the darkness wondering if she was going mad.

* * *

The sun rose on another bright day and, to Mandy's relief, the ghosts of the night before were dispelled. He'd laid a trap, she'd weakened but seen the danger in time. The world was good again.

Renzo seemed to have forgotten about the night before. He had some words of advice for each of them.

To Mandy he said, 'Don't rush it. You climb as if you're always trying to prove something. Just take it easy.'

They all set out cheerfully, taking deep breaths of the clear air, relishing the day to come.

As they trod carefully along a narrow ridge, Mandy began to fantasise about reaching the top. How incredibly blue the sky was, how wonderful it would feel to be there! Entranced, she let her thoughts drift.

Suddenly the ground, so firm beneath her a moment ago, simply ceased to exist. For a blinding moment the steep slope stretched away, yawning into the depths of infinity. Snow and sky became one, swirling sickeningly back and forth. Then the world steadied again. She was being drawn upwards, supported around her waist by an arm that seemed to be made of steel.

'All right?' said Renzo's voice.

She lay on her back, looking up into the

heavens, her heart thundering, while the universe fell into its right place again.

'What happened?' she gasped.

'You slithered, but it's all right now,' he said in a reassuring voice. 'Take a few deep breaths. No rush.'

'I'm fine,' she said, sitting up.

She began to get determinedly to her feet, accepting his support for a few moments. As they went on she put a brave face on it, but she felt shaken and it was a relief when Renzo said, 'We're not going so far today. There's another hut soon up ahead. It's not as grand as the one I was aiming for, but it'll give us a much-needed rest.'

Mandy was desperately glad. Weariness had caught up with her and there was a pain in her leg where she'd scraped it as she'd fallen. At last the hut came into view. As Renzo said, it was basic, but comfortable.

In the bedroom, shared by four girls, Joan took charge of Mandy, helping her to undress and getting out her nightwear, a pair of pyjamas, consisting of a jacket and shorts, which revealed a long red mark down her calf.

'Wow!' Joan exclaimed.

'It's impressive, isn't it?' Mandy said, touching it gently. 'It's also sore.'

There was a knock at the door and Renzo's voice said, 'Can I come in?'

'Yes, fine,' Joan called.

'Joan, Peter's looking for you,' he said, entering. 'I think he's planning a romantic tryst in the moonlight. Shall I tell him you're not interested?'

'Don't you dare,' Joan said eagerly and slipped away.

'Let me have a look at that leg,' Renzo said.

Mandy sat on the bed, swinging her legs up so that he could see the mark, and he seated himself, inspecting it critically and laying his hand over it.

'It'll be better when I've rubbed some of this in,' he said, holding up a bottle.

'What is it?'

'Dr Renzo's All Purpose Linctus is what you need. Stretch out.'

His manner was so impersonal that it was easy to lean back, close her eyes and succumb to the soothing effect of his hands rubbing her leg rhythmically. It was wonderfully relaxing, and she soon felt warmth flowing through her.

'Mmm!' she said softly.

'Good?'

'Mmmm!'

'Got any more aches and pains?'

'Everywhere,' she murmured. 'Neck, shoulders, arms, back—'

'Turn over.'

She did so and he continued massaging her back, sliding his hands under the cotton jacket until, almost without realizing what she was doing, she opened the buttons at the front and he pulled it off.

How good it felt to have him massaging her spine, her shoulders, her neck, driving the strain away until she was floating in a cocoon of comfort. She was vaguely aware that she was being foolish, lying here, half naked, alone with a man who charmed his way through life. When he'd finished easing her ailments he would try once more to bring her under his spell, perhaps to avenge his defeat the night before.

He'd do it by letting his hands wander just a little too far, drifting forwards to caress her breasts, pausing to see if she objected, but not really expecting it. Then she would have to be firm with him, which would be hard because she felt too contented to be firm about anything.

'Right, that should do it,' Renzo said, standing up. 'I'll send some food in, and then a good night's sleep should make you feel better. Goodnight.'

And he was gone.

Mandy lay there, thoughtful, unsure whether to credit him with being a gentleman or blame him for the implied slight. While she was trying to decide, she fell asleep.

CHAPTER THREE

WHEN she awoke, Joan was there.

'Renzo sent me in with food an hour ago, but you were dead to the world,' she said. 'Now, I'm under strict orders to keep an eye on you and make sure you eat as soon as you awake.'

Mandy sat up, rubbing her eyes. 'Where does he get off giving people orders?'

'He doesn't, really. He just gets his own way with that smile. It's far more effective than anything else, sort of wicked and gorgeous. It invites you into a conspiracy with him, and you know that it would be the most delightful conspiracy in the world.'

Now Mandy knew what she had against him.

'Does Peter know you feel like that about our great and glorious leader?' she asked tartly.

'Every girl on this trip feels like that about him. Except you, but then you're just "ornery". I can't think why, especially when he's been so nice to you today. Oh, yes—I see. I should have thought of that.'

'Thought of what?'

'When he was giving you that massage—I should have stayed here, shouldn't I? I thought he was the perfect gentleman, but I ought to have known better.'

'What are you saying?' Mandy demanded.

'Well—you know—he probably let his hands wander too far. That's it, isn't it? He "took advantage of you".'

'No, he didn't,' Mandy said, exasperated beyond endurance. 'He was totally professional and his hands didn't wander one inch from where they should be.'

'What, not even the tiniest—'

'*No!*'

'Ah,' said Joan wisely. 'Now I see.'

'There's nothing to see. It's time I got up,' Mandy said firmly. 'I'll eat out there. Shall we go?'

Joan's knowing eyes saw too much.

Mandy edged tentatively off the bed, fearing the worst, but she felt good. Dr Renzo had been very effective, she thought, pulling on some clothes, pleased to find that it was easy.

The others raised a cheer as she appeared and asked kindly how she was. Renzo didn't speak, but he observed her carefully and served her food with his own hands.

'Eat it all,' he said. 'You've got to keep your strength up.'

While she ate he watched over her like a guard dog, or a nanny. Suddenly her thoughts about his amorous intentions seemed ridiculous, and she began to chuckle.

'Careful,' he said gently. 'What's so funny?'

'Nothing—nothing—' she gasped.

'Well, don't choke yourself for nothing. Steady.' He was patting her on the back. 'That's better. Now can you share the joke?'

'No way,' she said. 'Some jokes just can't be shared.'

'They can be the best,' he suggested.

'That's true, and this one— Oh, don't get me started again.'

He looked at her curiously, and seemed about to say something, when a shout of, *'Hey!'* made everyone look up.

It was Henry, standing at the window.

'It's snowing,' he bawled.

At once they crowded to the window to see the soft flakes drifting down. Renzo slipped outside and Mandy joined him.

'I don't like this,' he said, staring intently.

'It's not very bad, is it?' she asked. 'It's only a light fall.'

'Yes, but if it keeps on for long it can have a destabilising effect. You get too much light, powdery snow that hasn't had a chance to firm up and compact with the rest.'

'You mean, we couldn't go on?'

'It might be a good idea to turn back.'

'I hope we don't have to,' she said with a little sigh. 'It's so lovely up here—and just a little bit of snow—'

'The trouble with you English is that you live in a moderate climate,' he chided her. 'You don't really understand that snow can be dangerous. But look high up.' Renzo indicated the flakes and, beyond them, the white peaks rearing up in the darkness. 'Snow like that isn't just affecting life. It *is* life. At the best it's a challenge, at the worst it's an enemy.'

'Hey ho! That's that then.'

'No, it's too soon to know how bad it'll be. Don't despair yet.'

'Me, I never despair,' said a voice behind them, and they both groaned at the arrival of Henry. 'Come on,' he rallied them. 'Where's your sense of adventure?'

'I put it to rest on the day I accepted responsibility for bringing people up here,' Renzo said through gritted teeth.

Now he was a guard dog again, shepherding them both back inside, commanding everyone to bed, chivvying them until they obeyed.

'How's the leg?' he asked Mandy.

'Fine. Everything's fine. Dr Renzo's Linctus is great. You should patent it.'

'No, I keep it for special occasions. Sleep well.'

To everyone's relief, the snow stopped during the night, but the day was overcast, making Renzo frown. As breakfast finished they were startled by the sight of a group coming out of the clouds on skis, heading towards them. When they arrived, it soon appeared that they had turned back.

'It's getting bad up ahead,' said the leader, a bearded young man called Toby. 'We're going down before it gets worse.'

'Right, then so will we,' Renzo declared. 'Sorry, folks, but safety first.

'Everyone get packed up and ready to go. And that includes you, Henry. Henry? Where is he?'

'I haven't seen him this morning,' one of the men said.

Even then nobody guessed the truth. Renzo simply shrugged and said, 'Tell him to get packed up, and then hurry.'

It was another five minutes before one of the

young men approached him and said worriedly, 'Henry's vanished. We found this.'

It was a note in Henry's schoolboy hand-writing:

Some of us aren't afraid to go on. See you up there, losers!

'He's gone ahead on his own!' Mandy breathed. 'How can he be such an idiot?'

'Because he *is* an idiot,' Renzo said savagely.

The look on his face made his audience recoil. They were used to seeing Renzo friendly, amusing and firm, but nothing had prepared them for the bleak fury that confronted them now.

'Scary,' somebody muttered.

Mandy agreed. Suddenly he become a new man, one capable of terrible deeds. She wondered how she could ever have thought him lightweight.

He began to curse in Italian, speaking softly but in a way that made the underlying violence more alarming. At last he controlled himself and said, 'I have to go after him. The rest of you are going down with the party that's just arrived. Get moving.'

Nobody felt inclined to argue with him in this

mood. Mandy slipped into the bedroom and packed up her things ready for departure. A resolution was growing in her. She couldn't tell from whence it came, but instinctively she knew that she must not let Renzo go after Henry alone.

'Are you ready?' Renzo asked when she appeared.

'Yes, but I'm not going down. I'm coming up with you.'

'No way. That fool could do anything.'

'Then you might be glad of backup,' she said defiantly.

'Look, I don't know what's going to happen, but he's capable of landing us all at the bottom of a ravine.'

'Fine, I'll let you tackle him, and if he takes you down with him, I'll still be alive to tell the world what happened to you.'

He stared at her, speechless.

'Look,' she persisted, 'I'm coming whether you like it or not. I can either go with you in relative safety, or I can go on my own and take my chances.'

'Is there any use saying no to you?' he snapped.

'None at all, so why are we wasting time?'

Joan and Peter emerged at that moment and Renzo appealed to them. 'Can you talk some sense into her? She thinks she's coming with me.'

'Great idea,' Joan said. 'I'll come too to keep an eye on her.'

'Me too,' Peter said.

Renzo tore his hair. 'When we get out there, you do as I tell you, and if we see Henry, you stay clear.'

Toby was gathering his party ready for departure, asking if anyone was joining them. Mandy, Joan and Peter folded their arms stubbornly, but the rest trooped out, ready to descend the mountain. There were goodbyes all round, and then Renzo was left alone with the other three.

'You're mad, all of you,' he growled.

'Yup, you're stuck with us,' Mandy affirmed. 'Some people would call it loyalty.'

'Most people would call it stupidity.' But his face softened as he said, 'Thank you.'

As the others busied themselves with final preparations, Renzo moved closer to Mandy, murmuring, 'You haven't got the infernal nerve to try and protect me, have you?'

'What, delicate little me?' she teased. 'No, the one I'm trying to protect is Henry—from you.'

'You might have a point there.'

They fitted on their skis, Renzo checked the ropes that connected them, and they set out, climbing slowly and carefully, their eyes skinned for any sign of Henry.

'It's a pity we can't shout,' Joan observed. 'I've got plenty of names I'd like to call him.'

'Don't,' Renzo said firmly. 'If there's any name-calling to be done *I'll* do it, at close quarters.'

But the day moved on without any sight of their quarry. Mandy hoped fervently that he was safe, but only for Renzo's sake. If one of his party came to harm he would get the blame, however wrongly. She felt a powerful surge of anger towards Henry.

It grew colder and bleaker as they climbed. Now there was no sun and the world was grey. Peter, whose courage was fast deserting him, was the first to express doubts.

'I wouldn't mind finding a hut right now.'

'What about that one over there?' Joan said, pointing in the distance.

'It's deserted,' Renzo said. 'Can you see that it's on the edge of a precipice? It wasn't on the edge when it was built, but the ground has fallen away ever since, until it's no longer safe.'

They moved on up, anxiety growing on them, until suddenly Renzo said, 'I can see him.'

Henry was up ahead on a ridge, turning to watch them, waving like a victor.

'Damned fool!' Renzo snapped. 'He's actually pleased with himself.'

Henry was dancing up and down, a mad manikin in the growing shadows. 'Come on,' he called. 'It's great up here.'

'You come down,' Joan called back.

'Hush,' Renzo said frantically. 'Don't you know better than to shout in these mountains? Do you want to start an avalanche?'

'Hi!' bawled Henry from the ridge. 'Come on up.'

'Stay here,' Renzo said. 'I'm going to get him. Don't make any loud noises.'

He disconnected the rope that linked him to Mandy and began to head up the slope, while Henry danced and shouted.

'He really is going to cause trouble,' Peter said.

As if to confirm it, there was a soft rumble from the distance. Although little more than a sigh, it had a threatening sound in this place where silence was normal.

'I'm getting out of here,' said Peter. 'Let's go, Joan. Mandy?'

'We can't just abandon Renzo,' she objected. 'He knows what he's doing.'

'He might, but Henry doesn't. Joan—'

'Yes, I think I'll go too.'

'Mandy?'

'I'm staying here,' she insisted. For her, there was no real decision to be made.

'OK. See you around.'

In moments the others had uncoupled themselves from her and hurried away. Up ahead, Mandy could see Henry beginning to ski down until he reached Renzo. Even at this distance she could tell that he was on a 'high'.

She began to move up to join them, arriving just in time to hear Henry say, 'You've got no sense of fun, man.'

'The thing about fun is that you need to be alive to enjoy it,' Renzo said, quietly firm. 'Now shut up and come down with us.'

Henry made a face behind his back, looking to Mandy for silent support. But she shook her head. He glared and when Renzo tried to hook him up to the rope that would connect them he backed off hurriedly.

'No way. I'll go down but I'm damned if I'm going to be tied to you.'

'Stop fooling about,' Renzo demanded.

'I mean it. *Just keep away from me.*' He said the last words on a shout, skiing away fast.

'Let's go,' Renzo muttered.

He connected her to the rope and they began the descent. Mandy heard the swift rushing noise of the skis on the snow. The sound seemed to build up in her ears, growing more ominous until she realized that she was listening to something different—something terrifying. The snow was moving.

Suddenly the movement was everywhere—behind her, beside her, around her, growing louder.

'*Renzo!*' she shrieked.

'We must get ahead of it,' he shouted. 'Quick as you can! *Don't do that!*'

The shout was jerked from him as she glanced over her shoulder and saw the snow sweeping down on them, faster every moment, thundering, threatening. She knew in that instant that they would never escape it, but she skied on, still roped to Renzo, feeling him draw her forwards in a frantic attempt to outrun the danger.

Then thought stopped, sensations ceased to be separate and blended into one storm of fear and horror. The whole world was white, above and below her, behind and in front. Nothing but white existed. Nothing ever had or ever would again.

She didn't see the wall that loomed up behind the white, didn't know it was there until she slammed into it. Her skis hit first, saving her from some of the impact. Even so, she was left breathless and half stunned. A scream of fear and dread broke from her and she looked around frantically.

'Renzo! *Renzo! Where are you?*'

'Here.' His voice reached her from a few inches away but she couldn't see him underneath the snow.

'Where are you? Oh, God!'

To her desperate relief, she felt his hand groping out of the snow to touch hers, seize it firmly.

'It's all right,' he said hoarsely. 'Don't panic, we're at the hut I showed you. If we can get inside, we'll be safe. Try to move towards me.'

It was hard to move with her skis impeding her but, with him drawing her towards him, she finally managed it, parting the snow until she could just see him.

'The door's just to my left,' he said. 'Let's hope it isn't locked.'

For once, luck was with them. After rattling the door for a moment, Renzo managed to get it open, but at once snow began to pour in through the gap.

'We have to get in fast,' he said, almost dragging her sideways and through the door. *'Push!'* he yelled.

Together they shoved hard, pushing the door closed with agonizing slowness, forcing the threatening snow back and back until they had defeated it, at least for the moment.

'Thank God!' he gasped. 'It's a heavy door. It should hold.'

'Does that mean we're safe?'

'Of course we are. We can hole up here until they find us, which shouldn't be long.'

As he spoke he gave her a bright smile, and its very cheerfulness told her that he didn't believe a word he was saying. They were trapped, perhaps for days, perhaps for ever.

But this wasn't the time for talk. There was too much to be done.

'Let's get these awkward things off,' he said, beginning to pull at his skis. 'Mandy? What's the matter?'

'Just a minute,' she choked. 'I just—'

'Here, sit down,' he said, guiding her to a sofa, making her sit down and kneeling to remove her skis. Then he sat beside her and put his arm around her. 'All right, give yourself time.'

She was shaking violently, tears pouring down her face.

'They're dead,' she cried. 'They must be dead—Joan and Peter, Henry—they're out in the open—they must be swept away—'

'We don't know that,' he tried to soothe her. 'Mandy, Mandy—'

Renzo pulled her against himself in a big hug, then rocked back and forth, murmuring soothing words and stroking her hair. But nothing could stop the tears. Submerged in agony, she flailed her arms, thumping him fiercely.

'They're dead—they're dead—' she screamed. 'Let me go.'

Mandy was struggling to free herself, taking him by surprise so that she was out of his arms before he could stop her. Now she was running here and there in an agony of grief and guilt, colliding with walls, recoiling, running again she knew not where, anywhere if only she could flee the horror inside her head.

He reached for her but she evaded him, heading for a door that led she knew not where. In her blind urgency to escape, she flung it open, not hearing Renzo's hoarse cry of, *'No!'* and was halfway across the floor of the room before she realized that the far wall had completely vanished.

Something thundered into her from behind, knocking her to the floor, landing on her, keeping her pinned down while she peered over into the abyss.

'All right, I've got you,' Renzo said. 'Just edge back slowly.'

She couldn't move. Her eyes were fixed on the endless drop into which she had nearly pitched headlong.

'Gently, gently,' Renzo urged, pulling her

inch by inch until she was a little way back from the edge. Then he seized her suddenly, yanking her to her feet and back through the door, which he slammed shut, then stood leaning back against it, holding her.

'That…was a very silly thing to do,' he said in a voice that shook.

'I…didn't know…'

'No, you can't see that side from where we were. I should have warned you.'

She began to calm down. 'How could you have warned me? What chance did you have? I was the idiot.'

'Mandy,' he murmured against her hair, 'are we going to pick this moment to argue about who's the idiot?'

'No, I guess it's not a very good idea,' she whispered.

'Come on, let's go somewhere safer.'

He drew her away into another part of the hut, where they could no longer see that the building was half gone, could almost pretend that it wasn't so.

The place was small and basic, but looked as if it had once been comfortable, and the rooms at the back were still serviceable.

'Everyone got out six months ago,' Renzo said. 'When they knew the place was unsafe they started removing furniture, but then there was a sudden lurch closer to the edge and they ran for it. Since then some more of the land has fallen away and taken the front of the hut with it. But we'll be safe here for a few days.'

'But how will we get out? We can't go forward or back.'

'When something like this happens the rescue service sends out helicopters. It may take a while but they'll find us, because I'm going to use the radio to let them know we're here. I'd better contact them now and tell them to look out for the others.'

But when he took the radio from his pack it lay useless in his hands, refusing to respond as he urgently pressed buttons.

'It's dead, isn't it?' she asked gently. 'But we each have a cellphone.'

'Let's try them, although I'm not sure if the signal can get through here.'

He was right. Neither phone was any use.

'It doesn't matter,' Renzo said firmly. 'The ones who went down ahead of us will tell them our rough direction. People get rescued all the time.'

'Yes, but—'

'Mandy, I've been in bad situations before. I've even given up hope and then found I was mistaken. We have a lot going for us. This hut is protecting us. If they don't find us we can survive here until the weather improves.'

'But how do we get out of the door?'

'We claw our way through the snow if we have to. Trust me, I know what to do.'

But, as if to defy his bravado, a vibration seemed to go through the hut. For a moment everything shuddered, almost as though the frail structure had lurched closer to the edge. Instinctively, she reached out to him and felt his arms close tightly about her.

No more pretence now, just the two of them seeking refuge in the only place it existed.

'It's all right,' he murmured against her hair. 'I'm here. It's going to be all right.'

And now she could believe it, simply because he said it. It made no sense, and yet it made every sense.

'Now,' he said with an attempt at cheerfulness, 'let's concentrate on what's urgent—getting settled, keeping warm, finding something to eat.'

'Right,' she agreed, knowing that there was nothing to do but follow his lead.

The darkness was total. Night had fallen outside, and no moonlight could reach them through the snow piled at the windows. Only the rooms directly over the abyss were moonlit, and they avoided them.

There was no heating and none of the lights worked, but luckily Renzo's torch still functioned and by its beam they managed to explore a little. There was a bathroom, with water still on tap from a tank outside, and finally the kitchen. There they found bottles of water and some glasses.

'And canned food,' Renzo observed. 'Thank goodness they didn't have time to remove this. We won't starve, although the cuisine may be a rather weird mixture.'

Still using the torch, they groped around to find a table and two chairs.

'I don't know what this is,' Renzo said, opening a can. 'Cross your fingers.'

Using this principle they created a make-shift meal consisting of custard and fruit pieces, washed down by bottled water. As they ate he talked, reassuring her, trying to make this sound like a normal day, until at last she whispered, 'Don't. Please don't.'

'All right,' he said. 'We ought to get some rest anyway. We've both had the stuffing knocked out of us.'

She didn't press him further. There was no knowing how deep was the snow that held them trapped, or how solidly it was frozen. Their chances of survival were poor, and in his heart she guessed he knew this, and suspected that she knew it, as well.

But it was too soon to confront that prospect.

Only one bedroom was left, with two narrow beds, a foot apart. Fully dressed, they fell into these and pulled the blankets up to their ears.

'Goodnight,' Renzo said.

'Goodnight.'

With the lights out she might almost have thought that everything was fine, except for the cold that made her huddle up. She wondered if Renzo was cold in the other bed.

If you let your thoughts dwell on the reality you could go mad, she thought. Because reality wasn't reality. What was happening was impossible, so it wasn't really happening at all. It was only in her head that the snow was all around, which meant that if she thought hard she could make it go away—only it wouldn't go away, no matter how frantically she—

'Mandy, Mandy, wake up!' She thought that was Renzo's voice but she couldn't hear him properly because someone was screaming. 'Mandy, hush, hush!'

Then she knew it was herself screaming, but she couldn't stop until he drew her close, burying her face in his shoulder until she fell silent.

'OK, OK, are you awake now?'

'Yes,' she choked, clinging to him.

At last she stopped shivering and he released her, just a little.

'You were having a nightmare,' he said softly. 'I'm not surprised, but don't worry, it won't be much longer.'

'Renzo, you don't have to tell me kind lies,' she said quietly. 'I can take the truth.'

'We could still be rescued—'

'I know. But there's every chance that we won't be, and that's a fact.'

He grew very still, not answering but holding her close, and a feeling of contentment spread over her. It was incredible in the circumstances but it was as though his arms had the power to fend off disaster. She found she could even manage a mild joke.

'You don't have to protect me. I'm not really that delicate, you know.'

'No, I guess you never were,' he murmured. 'You tried to tell me, but I wouldn't listen, would I? That's the way I am. I believe some people find me intolerable because of it.'

'Tell me who they are and I'll go after them,' she said at once. 'I won't let anyone bad-mouth you.'

He laughed against her hair. 'That's all right,

then. With you to defend me, what could I have to fear?'

'Don't let go of me,' she said. 'Stay here.'

'Wait a minute.'

He drew away, returned to his own bed and pushed it up against hers.

'That's better,' he said, taking her in his arms again.

Now it was easy to drift back to sleep, and this time there were no nightmares.

CHAPTER FOUR

WHEN Mandy awoke she was alone. With the window blocked by snow, she had no idea of the time and groped her way cautiously out of the room and across the hall until she could see the open door that led to the 'forbidden' room, the one whose far wall was missing, and the only place where there was any light.

There she found Renzo, looking out onto the snow that was still falling heavily.

'If a helicopter comes up here, this is the best place to wave,' he said as she edged cautiously close to him.

'Has there been any sign of a helicopter?'

'No, and even if there were—'

'They couldn't see us through that snow,' she finished.

'Let's get something to eat. Then we'll come and stand guard.'

They spent the day in the forbidden room,

sitting well back, listening for the sound of a helicopter that never came. By the time the snow stopped, darkness had fallen and they moved back to the safe part of the house to find something to eat by torchlight.

'You're cold,' he said as she shivered. 'There's only one place to keep warm, and the sooner we're there the better.'

Before they got under the blankets, he tried his cellphone again, then hers. Neither gave any response. Mandy sensed his despair, and put her arms around him.

'It doesn't change what we already know,' she said softly.

'I wanted to make you safe. Some guide I am!'

'I am safe.'

He turned his head. 'I wish I could see your face,' he murmured.

'It's the same as always.'

'No, it's changed. *You've* changed.'

'Perhaps. Let's get warm.'

They lay down, pulling the blankets up and lying wrapped in each other's arms, as close as possible, to share their bodies' warmth.

'If we could have got through on the phone,' he said at last, 'do you have anyone to call? I mean, anyone who'll worry about you.'

'Not really. I've only got distant family, that

I never see. I don't mean that we've quarrelled, but they're scattered all over the country.'

'Friends? Lovers?'

'Lovers, plural? Don't be cheeky.'

She imagined him giving her a quirky grin. 'Just one, then?'

'No, I'm done with love. It's a bore and a waste of time.'

'Ah, yes, you mentioned him before, the one who wanted "something to get hold of".'

'I thought he was delightful at first. He could make me laugh, and that's a big plus.'

'Yes, it is,' he said thoughtfully.

'And you'd know, wouldn't you? Make 'em laugh and then it's off to bed. I used to watch him at parties, looking around him like the beacon from a lighthouse, calculating how long it would take to bring them under his spell.'

'And that—' In his indignation he propped himself on his elbow. 'You think I'm like that? It's what you've always had against me, isn't it? He treated you badly and I get the blame. Woman, may you be forgiven! But not by me.'

'Don't give me the innocent act,' she chided. 'You and him might have come from the same mould. I've seen you look around the room in the same way.'

'I won't deny that I've had my moments—'

'Ahh!'

'But not on this kind of trip. Believe what you like, but I don't try to seduce the girls in a party that I'm leading. For one thing, it would be unprofessional, and for another, their boyfriends would kill me. I'd end up down the nearest crevasse.'

'You prefer a balcony to swing from?'

She heard his laugh in the darkness, and felt the vibration of his body.

'All right, all right,' she conceded. 'You're Mr Virtuous.'

'Not entirely. There is one girl I had trouble being virtuous with. She always left me wondering, you see, and I could never work out whether she was tantalizing me on purpose, or just didn't know how she was getting under my skin.'

She felt his lips close to her ear as he murmured, 'I'll never know, unless you tell me.'

'What did you—' Astounded by what she'd heard, she turned her head and found his lips brushing her cheek. Coming unexpectedly, it was like an electric shock. 'What did you say?'

'Did you know what you were doing to me? It's kind of important to me to know.'

'What *I* did to *you*? Haven't you got that the wrong way round?'

'Not at all. From the start, you set out to be a thorn in my side. The first day was all right. We had that chat in the evening and I thought, This is great. Here's someone I can talk to. But after that you were possessed by the devil, and I think you did it on purpose.'

She recovered her poise enough to say, 'Couldn't you tell?'

'No, that's what I meant. I never knew. I still don't know and it's driving me wild. You're such a little tease—'

'I am not!'

'Really? So it was just accident that you danced like that with Marcel, knowing it would put everything you have on display.'

'I was decently dressed in trousers.'

'It wasn't your clothes, it was the way you moved—slinky, sensual, in tight trousers that showed you off to every man.'

'Including you?'

'You're damn right, including me. And when we were outside you lured me on to kiss you, then backed off, leaving me looking a fool— and feeling one.'

'Now wait a minute! It was you who lured me on, just to prove that no woman was immune to you, not even me. You admitted it.'

'I did what?'

'You said, "since you saw through me so easily…I might as well give up."'

'Well, of course I did!' he exploded. 'I had to say I hadn't been serious, to save my face. I was going crazy wanting to kiss you, but you'd just been leading me up a blind alley and having a good laugh.'

'And that's just what you were doing. Making a point.'

'Give me patience. I was the victim there.'

'Well, you got your revenge, didn't you, the next night,' she countered.

'What in heaven's name did I do the next night? You were poorly, I massaged you to make you better. And I never put a hand out of place, so why are you complaining?'

'*Because* you never put a hand out of place,' she said furiously.

'Did you want me to?'

'Give me patience! It's like trying to get through to a brick wall. Something stares you in the face and you can't see it. *And what's funny?*' Renzo had given a snort of laughter.

'I'm sorry,' he said in a shaking voice. 'It's you talking about seeing what's staring me in the face. Can you see anything?'

The darkness was black around them, but in her indignation she'd actually forgotten it. Now she was seized with longing to see him, but all she could do was reach out, touching his face, feeling the amusement that shook his body.

Had there ever been a man like this one? They were teetering on the edge of annihilation and he was *laughing*.

'I don't need to see you,' she said. 'I know you've got that wicked look, and you're making fun of me—'

'Making fun? After what you've put me through? Mandy—'

His voice changed as her fingertips brushed his lips.

'Mandy…Mandy…*Mandy!*'

The last word was muffled as his lips touched hers in the kiss that had always been waiting for them, and had taken too long. Now she could be honest with herself and admit how badly she'd wanted this. His mouth was just as she'd known it would be—strong and generous, teasing, coaxing, silently imploring her to respond wholeheartedly.

There was no resisting that plea and she yielded to it with joy, moving her lips against his until his urgency overwhelmed her and she opened to him, letting him entice her with his tongue. He was as skilled as she'd known he would be, and at one time—a few days and a thousand years ago—she would have resented that skill. Now she revelled in it, answering with flickering movements of her own tongue, in an echo of the duelling that had always been how they communicated.

They were moving their hands, touching each other wherever they could reach, frustrated by the thick clothes they were wearing. But the need to be naked with him was greater than any cold, and she began pulling open her zips and buttons.

'Careful, it's freezing,' he muttered, but he was fumbling with his own clothes as he spoke.

They helped each other undress and went completely under the blankets to escape the icy air. She could feel him beneath her fingers, lean yet muscular, full of tensile strength, exploring her as she was exploring him.

At first she was tentative, learning about the man even as she learned about his body. But suddenly she discovered that everything she did was right, because a thrill went through him, so intense that she felt it herself, and he said fiercely, 'Do that again, don't stop—*don't stop!*'

'I'm not going to,' she said joyfully, redoubling her efforts and feeling him respond with vigour.

Mandy had known desire before but never like this, the feeling heightened by the fast approach of the unknown, sweeping her up, filling her with the desperate desire to experience this while there was still time.

And it was the same with him, she knew beyond a doubt. Life couldn't end until he'd known this pleasure, this joy. From the start there had been a connection between them, starting in their minds, reaching out to their emotions and finishing with their sensations, where it clamoured for release. Now it was having its way, driving them like one entity hurtling towards the same end.

She never knew if he moved over her or if she pulled him over. She knew only that she had to have this, to have him, inside her, filling her, encompassing her, offering her the last gift she would ever know. She returned everything with all her heart, seeking to give him even more than he gave her, but knowing it was impossible, because he gave everything from a generous heart. And she should always have known that this was the truth about him, but she hadn't, until it was too late.

Then they lay together, arms entwined, basking in the warmth of each other's bodies, but even more in the warmth of the heart.

'Are you all right?' Renzo whispered, but then gave a suppressed choke. 'Listen to me.

I'm going off my head. In a few hours—well, anyway, it was a stupid question.'

Mandy tightened her arms about him. 'You're not going off your head. Not while I'm here. And, if you are, we'll go off together. Now I'm talking nonsense.'

She too began laughing wildly, clinging to him, feeling him holding on to her as though she was all that was left in the world. And it was true. There was nothing but this; no snow or danger lurking in wait. Just warmth and joy because he was there, and he was hers.

But then prosaic matters intruded and she muttered, 'Let's do something before we freeze to death.'

They scrambled back into their clothes before groping their way to the cupboard, yanking out every blanket they could find and tossing it all on the bed. Then they dived under the covers again and huddled together.

'You know,' she mused, 'in the fantasies he seduces her on satin sheets. She's wearing diaphanous lingerie and he draws it slowly away, piece by piece. Then she does the same for him, overwhelmed by his perfect taste in clothes.'

'That's true,' he said gravely. 'Yanking off three layers of flannel and a pair of long woollen underpants doesn't quite do it.'

'It did it for me,' she said contentedly, snuggling against him.

Mandy nodded off almost at once and slept without nightmares, only peace.

In the morning they took some breakfast from the fast declining food stock and ate it the forbidden room where they could watch the falling snow. There was a little light, so that they didn't have to waste the torch batteries.

'The snow's hypnotic, isn't it?' she said. 'It almost sends you back to sleep.'

Dreamily she began to recite a few lines from a poem about snow.

'Did you write that?' Renzo asked.

'No, I learned it at school when I was ten.'

'And you still know it? What a memory. I can't get over you being an academic.'

'Because I don't look like one? Don't you know by now not to judge by appearances?'

'Are you going to throw "delicate" at me again?' he asked warily.

'No, I promise. Actually, at one time I wanted to be a dancer. I took lessons, but I wasn't good enough to make a career of it, so I found something else.'

'So that's why you move as you do, like a pretty little cat?'

She smiled. 'That's what you say now, but the first time you called me a cat it wasn't a compliment.'

'Not entirely, but I've always been fascinated by your movements, and I don't just mean when you were dancing. Everything you do is graceful, like an elegant feline, insinuating herself wherever she wants to be. You insinuated yourself into my mind. At first I didn't want you there, but you wouldn't go away.'

'That's me. Awkward. Never did what I was supposed to do.'

'I'll second that.'

'Cheeky!'

He hugged her, resting his cheek on her head.

'You're so tiny,' he complained. 'I keep being afraid you'll slip through my fingers.'

'You'll have to hold on to me tightly then, won't you?'

'Let's get inside. There are easier ways to hold you tightly.'

Once under the covers, they went on talking.

'Do you really not have any family?' he asked.

'Only the distant ones I told you about.'

'Cat? Dog?'

'Nope, just one very good friend. Her name's Sue. We were at school together and we've stayed close, although we don't meet much.

She's a nurse, working in the north. Sometimes she gets down to London and stays with me.'

'And that's all? It sounds lonely. Is it enough for you?'

'In many ways, yes. I love my work, and sometimes it feels like all I need.'

'But not always?'

'Well, I'd like more eventually…one day…'

Mandy fell silent as she realized what she was saying. 'One day' would never come. With every passing moment that grew more certain.

'What would you like—one day?' he asked gently.

'Someone of my own, who was just mine, who saw only me, thought of only me, wanted only me.' She made a sound of impatience with herself. 'That sounds so self-centred.'

'No, it's what we all want, if we're honest. It's just so hard to find, even impossible.'

'Impossible? You really think that?'

'I don't know. I always used to, but that was then. Now it's different. I don't know what I believe any more, except that I believe in you.'

'What about family? Is there anyone who'll worry about you?'

'Only my grandfather, but he's very old and he's mostly lost contact with the world.'

'No parents?'

'My mother left when I was about six. She and my father were a happy couple—so everyone thought. Then she fell in love with someone else and next thing, she was gone.'

'Leaving you behind?' she asked, aghast.

'I came home from school one day and she wasn't there.'

'What? She didn't explain or say goodbye—'

'She wanted her freedom,' Renzo said simply.

'Did you ever see her again?'

'Now and then. She eventually married her lover and they had three children.'

In her anger on his behalf she spoke without thinking. 'So she didn't want to be free of *them*?'

It was a moment before Renzo said quietly, 'No, just me.'

There was a lifetime of desolation and rejection in those three words.

Appalled, Mandy realized that she'd touched a nerve that still hurt after so many years.

'Bitch!' she exploded. 'I could kill her.'

Renzo's voice was shaky as he said, 'Hey, it's all right. It's all in the past.'

'Is it really in the past?'

'No, I guess not. It stays with you, but at this moment it doesn't seem important. Nothing that ever happened to me before counts beside you.'

She stroked his face. 'If we get out of this—'

He kissed her. 'You must stay with me, always.'

'Always and for ever.'

She held him tight and, after a moment, said, 'And your poor father. It must have broken his heart.'

'At first. After that, he embarked on what he called "a new life". I went to stay with Nonno as soon as I could.'

'Nonno? That's grandfather, isn't it?'

'That's right. Every time I visited my father, he seemed to have a different woman. He said variety was the spice of life. Once I reminded him of how crazy he'd been about my mother, and he didn't know what I was talking about. He's dead now.'

'And your mother?'

'Living in Australia—I think. I sensed that she felt uncomfortable when I visited, so I stopped bothering her.'

'Well, I guess it's no mystery why you don't think ties are the greatest thing in the world,' she seethed.

He grinned in self-mockery.

'I thought of a clever plan. I'd live as I pleased, do everything I wanted to do first. Then I'd get married and have children when I was too old and decrepit to do anything else.'

'There's a flaw in that plan,' Mandy said gravely.

'Yes, I'm beginning to see that. Besides, I soon realized that a man who takes such a jaundiced view of families as I do had probably better not have children.'

'But you might be a better parent because you've seen the other side,' she suggested.

'That's a nice theory, but I don't believe it. There's too much in there—' he laid a hand over his heart '—that had better stay well hidden.'

Silence: the contented silence of two people at ease with each other. Soon they would sleep, make love, rise again to eat, then return to bed and talk. And it dawned on her that this was how people behaved on honeymoon, which was the ultimate madness.

Going to the kitchen again was a worrying experience. The bottled water was running out. There was still the water in the tank, which wasn't really for drinking. Otherwise there was only a bottle of whisky. They surveyed it in silence.

'Not for me,' Mandy said. 'I don't want to hide. I want to be there and know about it— whatever happens.'

'You might find it easier…' he ventured.

'I don't want it to be easy. It matters too much.'

Renzo leaned forwards and kissed her

tenderly. 'I knew you'd say that. You're right. Just us. That's all we need.'

When they'd eaten their meagre rations there was nothing to do but seek the warmth that only the bed could offer. They made love again, knowing that time was slipping away, and it was as sweet and pleasurable as before, but now there was an added resonance. With every tender gesture, every invitation given and received, they said goodbye.

There was desire in each caress, but softened by infinite tenderness.

'I wish I could see your face,' he murmured. 'I want to see how you look at me.'

'But you know my face,' she whispered. 'You don't need to see it.'

'But which face? The one that teases me—'

'No, not that one.'

'Tell me.'

'Kiss me first…again…again…'

Her voice trembled into a soft moan as his lips moved from her mouth to her jaw, her neck, her breasts. She entwined her fingers in his hair, drawing him closer, the more deeply to relish the feel of his tongue flickering against her skin. She was drowning in sensation, as warm and comforting as it was passionate.

With all her being she tried to do the same

for him, giving from a full heart, taking perhaps the last chance to show him what he was to her, although even she didn't truly know that. What they might have shared would have been revealed over years together—fighting, making up, having children. Now it must all be experienced in a few moments, and she gave herself up to the sensation with all her heart.

Renzo sensed her feelings deep in himself and moved up to where her face was, just below his, still seeking something he needed to know. He found it in her eyes that glittered brightly enough for him to see and heard it in the long sigh of satisfaction that broke from her, telling him that she was ready, eager for their union.

As he entered her, she arched up against him, claiming him as her own and becoming his in the same moment. No matter what would happen tomorrow, they would have this one last triumphant assertion of life.

'I love you,' he said softly. 'It may be the last time I ever say it, and if so, I'm glad it's to you and nobody else. You are everything to me, and you will be everything, for however long we have—and afterwards.'

'I'm glad too,' she told him. 'I love you and, whatever happens now, I can take it because we had this, and it matters more than anything else ever has.'

'More than anything ever will,' he whispered.

He slept first, holding her against him, her head against his heart, listening to the soft beat, until finally she too slept.

Mandy awoke to find herself alone and went to find Renzo in the forbidden room, watching the falling snow. He turned and smiled at her, and she remembered that smile afterwards because it was almost the last she saw of him. As she moved towards him the building began to shake and a thunderous grinding roar came from beneath their feet.

'Get back,' he yelled.

But she was petrified, staring at the floor that began to disintegrate under her feet. The next moment she felt a violent push that sent her flying to the back of the room so that her head hit the wall.

Now she knew what was happening. The ground beneath them had collapsed again, taking with it the place where Renzo had been standing. But he was no longer there. His lunge towards her had taken him almost to safety, but not quite. The floor was slipping away, sloping too steeply for him to be able to fight it. He fought to grab hold of something, but everywhere was too slippery.

'Renzo,' she screamed, stretching out her arms desperately.

But it was too late. He was vanishing faster every moment.

'Renzo! No—'

His face was turned up to her, tortured with strain and horror as he reached vainly for her.

'Mandy!'

The sound faded even as he uttered it. He was going down, down, until she could no longer see him. From somewhere in the distance she heard a long agonised cry that faded as it sank into the depths, like a man descending into hell.

'No—please, God, no!'

Forgetting safety, she crawled back to the new edge, looking down into the abyss where there was only deadly whiteness. Scream after scream burst from her, echoing down into nothingness, and more screams until all the world echoed with them, and then it was over.

CHAPTER FIVE

ON THE Via Manzoni the buildings spoke of money. Here, in the most elegant part of Milan, there was an air of indulgence and reaching out comfortably to the neighbours. All except for one house, which had a bolted and barred appearance, suggesting, at least, someone who preferred not to be disturbed and, at worst, someone who hated the world.

Mandy paused outside to check that she'd come to the right address. It was hard to connect Renzo with the slightly grim aspect of this place, yet the paper in her hand assured her that this was where he lived. She raised her hand to ring the bell, then backed off and went instead to a small café just down the street.

You've lost your nerve, she told herself crossly as she sipped her coffee. *But then, it's been a long time. Two years since we found each other, loved each other, lost each other.*

*And so many things have happened since then.
I know I've changed, and he must have
changed too.*

It saddened her to think of him being different. She could see him now, giving her the old smile—teasing, yet tender and generous. Surely nothing could have altered that?

She caught a glimpse of herself in a mirror on the wall. It was like seeing a ghost, and in a strange way that was how she'd felt since the day she'd awoken in a hospital in Chamonix to the news that, while she had been rescued, Renzo was missing and probably dead. His death had been confirmed a few days later.

She'd returned to England in a daze of grief and tried to take up the threads of her life, although, after the love that had blazed briefly and been so cruelly snatched away, it felt little better than a half life.

But then, two years later—almost to the day—she'd picked up a newspaper and read:

*Avalanche Victim Wrongly Identified.
It now seems that the body identified as
Italian climber Lorenzo Danilo Ruffini,
following the Alpine avalanche nearly two
years ago, was actually another man of
similar appearance...*

She'd embarked on a determined quest, hiring a private detective who had soon been able to tell her, 'It took the rescue team a long time to find him, and then nobody thought he would live. His body had actually shut down with the cold but, against all the odds, they managed to bring him back.'

'How did he come to be wrongly identified?'

'There were two men missing, and the woman who did the identification was the wife of the other one. She couldn't face the fact that he was dead, so she simply denied that the body was his. Then she had a complete mental collapse, but recently she recovered enough to admit the truth.

'He now lives in Milan, where he owns a sports-equipment company. His physical recovery took a long time, and his mental recovery even longer—and both, I understand, are incomplete. In fact, they will probably never be complete.'

And now, here she was, having followed the trail to Milan. In a few moments she would see Renzo again and know if the dream she'd carried in her heart had any reality.

One thought troubled her. She hadn't sought him out before because she'd thought he was dead, but he seemed to have made no effort to find her. It could have been done easily through Pierre Foule's records, but he hadn't tried. Had she too been reported as dead? Or had he simply put her behind him?

No! Her heart denied it fiercely. He had said, 'I love you. You are everything to me, and you will be everything, for however long we have—and afterwards.'

She heard his words but more, she saw him, not shielded by darkness as he had been then, but as he had lived in her heart ever since—his eyes softened with tenderness, his voice deep with fervour as he proclaimed his love for ever.

The man she remembered had not turned his back. He loved her still, as she loved him. Anything else was impossible.

Today she would see him again and life would spring anew within her. He would look at her and his face would be transformed with a joy that echoed her own, and somehow they would find the way forward again.

At last she rose, determined not to be afraid, walked back to the house and rang the bell.

It was answered by a woman in her thirties. She had a distracted air, but she smiled politely.

'Does Signor Lorenzo Ruffini live here?' Mandy asked in Italian.

'Yes, but he doesn't want to be disturbed. I'm Lucia, his secretary. Is he expecting you?'

'No, he's not expecting me. At least…' a sudden vagueness overtook her '…I don't think he is.'

'What name shall I tell him?'

'Mandy Jenkins.'

'Does he know you?'

'I don't…really know.'

'Look, I don't think—'

'I'll wait. I don't care how long it takes.'

She was inside the door before Lucia could protest.

'You'd better come in then, but it could be a long wait. He's got an important appointment with a business associate—well, more of an enemy, really. Mind you, he seems to think everyone is an enemy these days.' Lucia added confidingly, 'He's going to carve him up. Ah, that must be him.'

The doorbell had rung again. Lucia admitted a squat individual with an expanding belly and a cunning face.

'Signor Vanwick?' she asked politely.

'*Mr* Vanwick,' the man declared grumpily in English. 'I've got no time for that Signor stuff.'

'Yes, *Mr* Vanwick. Follow me, please.'

She led him down the hall, Mandy following, and opened a door.

'Mr Vanwick, Signor Ruffini,' she announced and stood back quickly before she was brushed aside by Vanwick's advancing bulk.

Before the door closed they could just hear him growl, 'Now then, Ruffini, what's all this trouble about my bill?'

'Nice character,' Mandy said in English. 'Not a good advertisement for my country.'

'No problem,' Lucia said. 'In a few minutes he'll come out of that door, pale and shaking. He tried to cheat Signor Ruffini out of a million euros and now he's going to wish he hadn't. Nobody makes that mistake twice. *Mr* Vanwick is an unpleasant man but I feel sorry for him, getting on Signor Ruffini's wrong side.'

'You don't like Signor Ruffini?'

'I'm not sure. He's a good boss in many ways. When my mother was ill he gave me plenty of time off on full pay. But working for him can be tough. He snaps, barks orders and talks to people without looking at them.'

'And he's going to "carve him up"? Does he do that often?'

'When he has to. People think, because he's been so ill, that he's a soft touch, but they soon learn their mistake.'

The sound of a voice came from the next room. It had a hard, unforgiving quality that fell unpleasantly on the ear.

'That's him,' Lucia said with relish.

As if to demonstrate, there came a cry, of 'Lucia,' through the door. She hurried in, leaving the door wide. Mandy moved quietly to a place where she could catch a glimpse of Renzo, but at the last moment she stopped, suddenly reluctant.

For two years she'd carried the memory of a man who was delightful, sweet-natured and devil-may-care. Every moment he'd been there in her heart, gazing gently at her with eyes full of love.

Now she was filled with foreboding. His voice alone warned her of a change in him, but that was natural, she tried to reassure herself. Inside, he was still the same man and when he saw her he would smile with joyful recognition.

Mandy moved quietly to where she could peer through the gap, and beheld him for the first time in two years. And what she saw made her freeze.

For a moment she actually didn't recognize him. Who was this grim, tight-faced individual? How could he be the man who'd held her so tenderly on the mountain?

He was sitting behind a large desk, but

suddenly he got to his feet and began to pace the room, hectoring the man who was sitting there, listening uncomfortably.

Mandy had a good look at his profile as he turned and recognised the sharp nose and firm chin. This was Renzo and not Renzo.

He must have suffered, she told herself. That and two years had changed him, as it had changed her. Yet there was something about this grim caricature that smothered her first happiness on finding him, leaving behind only dismay and sadness.

She backed away quickly and was seated again when Lucia hurried out.

'Now he wants something else, quick as possible, only it's buried in the files—somewhere.'

'I'll hold the fort while you look,' Mandy said.

'Thanks. He might call for that.' She indicated a newspaper cutting on the desk and hurried away.

Mandy stayed listening to Renzo's voice coming from next door, trying to hear in its harshness some hint of the voice she remembered—resonant, teasing, full of life. But it was impossible. This could have been the voice of a machine.

But that would surely change when he

realized that she was there and the memories of their time together came surging back.

'Lucia, bring me that cutting.' The order was barked out.

She took the cutting and went next door, her heart beating with expectation, waiting for the moment when he saw her, the shock in his face, then the pleasure.

He was standing by the window, talking over his shoulder to the fat man who sat with a scowl on his face. Mandy made out the words, 'I don't know how you thought you'd get away with it, Vanwick. Do you think I don't read the paperwork, or did you think I couldn't understand it?'

'You're making too much of this,' Vanwick tried to say.

'When a man cooks the books to charge me double, I'll make of it what I like. Look at that newspaper cutting. It'll tell you how much I know.'

As Vanwick took the cutting Renzo turned and regarded him contemptuously. His eyes flickered over Mandy and away again. There was no recognition. Nothing. He might not even have seen her.

But, just for a moment, he glanced back. Was it there? A question? Is she, isn't she?

Then Vanwick spoke, trying to whine his way

out of trouble, but Renzo silenced him with a blast of cold fury, all the more frightening for being restrained. As he spoke he moved about the room, occasionally pausing. And now Mandy, sharply alert, noticed that he kept one hand behind him. And that hand was always holding on to something, out of Vanwick's sight.

Another glance at his face and she understood everything. He was in pain, suffering so badly that it was all he could do to stay on his feet.

Sit down, she told him silently. *Why can't you be sensible and sit down?*

Because I'm an awkward customer, he told her out of the past. *I have to do it my way. Anything else is just giving in.*

His hand was just visible, so that she saw the moment when it clenched violently and knew he was at the end of his tether. Suddenly he swayed. Quick as a flash, she moved in front of him and felt his hand grip her arm with frantic strength.

'Get out of here,' he told Vanwick.

'But what are you going to—'

'I'll tell you later what I'm going to do. In the meantime you can sweat. *Now get out!*'

Vanwick hurried away. As soon as the door was closed Renzo's grip grew more fierce and he leaned on her heavily from behind.

'A chair,' he said hoarsely.

She guided him carefully to the nearest chair and supported him with all her strength, so that she could ease him into it slowly.

'You should have a doctor,' she said.

'No, I just need a few minutes' rest while my back eases. Get me the pills in the desk drawer.'

She found them and poured him some water from a decanter. He gulped everything down and sat there, shaking.

'I still think you should—' she began, but he interrupted her sharply.

'Never mind what you think. If you're going to work here, you'll have to learn not to argue with me.'

'But I'm not going to work here.'

'Aren't you Lucia's new assistant?'

'No, I'm…just someone who happened to be here. Let's leave that until later. Can you rest in that chair? It looks a bit hard.'

'You're right. I need to get across the courtyard to the part of the building where I live.'

'Shall I fetch someone to help you?'

'No way. Do you think I want my staff knowing that I'm like this? Why do you suppose I threw Vanwick out?'

'You mustn't show weakness to an enemy, must you?'

'So you do understand that!'

'But your staff aren't enemies.'

'It's as dangerous to show weakness to employees as to enemies.'

'Well, as I'm neither—'

'No, you're a damned interfering woman, who has to stick her nose into other people's business but, now you've done it, you may as well be useful.'

Indignation made her speak without thinking. 'You're a real charmer, aren't you?'

Renzo turned his head quickly, his eyes meeting hers, while the words resonated between them. How often in the past had she accused him of charm?

And he must remember it now. How could he not?

'I can be,' he said at last. 'When I have something to gain.'

'Well, don't waste it on me,' she ordered him tartly. 'Just tell me what you want me to do.'

'Let me take your arm while we walk across to the other side.'

Mandy had to help him up, not looking at his face because she knew he would hate her to see it contorted in pain. Then he slipped his hand through her arm and made it to the door, leaning on her slightly.

They moved across the hall to another door

that led into a wide courtyard, beautiful with flowers and shrubs, where a gardener was working. Renzo beamed and called to him pleasantly, while the hand that gripped her tightened desperately.

'That door,' he said, pointing. 'Here's the key.'

She guided him through it and to a chair.

'Close the door,' he gasped. 'And lock it.'

An elderly woman appeared through the opposite door, horrified when she saw him. 'I told you what would happen if you overdid it,' she exclaimed.

Instead of barking at her, Renzo assumed a rueful expression. 'All right, Teresa, you knew best, as always. Just get me a whisky.'

'On top of those pills?' Mandy exclaimed. 'I don't know what they were, but if they're any good you shouldn't be drinking alcohol.'

'Cancel the whisky,' Renzo growled. 'I'll have it later.'

He lay back against the sofa, covering his eyes with his hand. Mandy watched him with pity, wanting to go to him but knowing this wasn't the time. There was so much to be said first, so much to be discovered. Did he have any memory of her at all?

Glancing around the room, she saw a wheel-chair standing by the far wall. She wondered how much time he spent in it. Clearly he could walk, but not very much, and she guessed he forced himself to his feet more often than he ought.

At last Renzo dropped his hand and found Mandy was sitting in front of him, where he could see her face clearly. For a moment they looked at each other.

'Do I know you?' he asked at last.

She tensed, feeling the question like a slap in the face.

'I'm not sure,' she said after a moment. 'Perhaps you do.'

'It was you, wasn't it—on the mountain?'

'Yes, it was me.'

'Then you really existed all the time? I wasn't certain. I had so many dreams and illusions— I've lived in limbo.'

'I thought you were dead,' she said softly.

His mouth twisted. 'I am dead. Can't you see?'

'You're not dead, you're just bad tempered,' she said, speaking lightly on purpose. 'But that's not surprising. From what I heard, you went through a terrible time—'

'For pity's sake, don't start being sweet and understanding,' he said in disgust. 'It makes me want to commit murder.'

'No change there, then. You and I often wanted to murder each other.'

'Yes, that bit's coming back. We were always quarrelling, weren't we?'

'Not quarrelling,' she said quickly, 'bickering.'

'Don't sugar it. I was probably just as much of an ill-tempered swine in those days.'

'No, you weren't. You liked your own way, but you laughed a lot.'

He gave a grunt. 'I don't remember.'

No, she thought sadly. This wasn't the man she'd known, but another man who couldn't even recall who he himself had been. For a dreadful moment she wanted to walk out and never come back.

But she ignored the impulse. It was too soon to give up hope.

'But you remember me?' she asked, a touch wistfully.

'Only in the sense that I knew I'd seen your face before—somewhere. When I was in hospital I had some strange dreams, and you were often there.'

'But you didn't know if I was real or some mad sprite conjured up to torment you?'

'Something like that. I'm beginning to understand now.'

'A mad sprite?'

'Definitely.'

He spoke forcefully, but couldn't suppress a wince of pain.

'Enough for now,' she said. 'We'll talk when you're feeling better.'

'Who says we will? You're very free about giving orders in my house. I want that whisky.'

'No whisky.'

'Be damned to you!'

'Anything you say. I'm awkward, interfering, overstepping the mark. But if you remember anything about me, that shouldn't surprise you.'

'You'll leave this house now if you've got any sense.'

'Oh, I never had any of that.'

'Just go anyway, will you?' he said in a harsh voice. 'Please go.'

Mandy almost ran out of the room. Despite her combative tone, her heart was breaking. She'd thought she was prepared for the worst, but the reality was more terrible than anything she'd foreseen.

Safe out of sight, she leaned back against the wall, tears streaming down her face, whispering, 'No, no…please…no, it can't be… It mustn't be… Oh, my love…my love…'

She put up her hands to hide her face and remained there, helpless with grief, until a soft touch on her arm made her glance up to see Teresa.

'This way,' Teresa said softly, drawing her away until they reached the kitchen.

Mandy collapsed into a chair at the table, laid her head down on her arms and sobbed without restraint. Teresa wisely left her to it while she got on with making coffee.

Finally Mandy managed to pull herself together and drink from the cup Teresa had laid by her elbow.

'I'm sorry,' she said huskily.

'Don't be sorry. Better this way.'

It was true. The explosion had left her with a sense of relief.

'I'm Mandy,' she said.

'Did you let him scare you? You shouldn't.'

'Aren't you scared?'

'Not me. I was working for his family when he was a little boy.'

'Were you here when his mother left?'

'You know about that? How?'

'He told me.'

'He *told* you that?' Teresa seemed thunder struck. 'He actually told you? But he never tells anyone. He doesn't talk about it—ever. He'd die first.'

'Maybe that's it. We were trapped together in

the avalanche, and he thought he was going to die. We both did.'

'So it was you,' Teresa said, looking at her shrewdly.

'How do you mean?'

'You were on that mountain with him.'

'Does he ever talk about me?' Mandy asked eagerly.

'It's the way he refuses to talk about you that's always made me wonder. He said there was someone there, but then he clammed up. I've never known whether she'd really gone from his mind, or whether he was trying to drive her away. He's been that way ever since his bitch of a mother left. He buries everything inside and there are things he won't let anyone speak of. I looked after him then, and I'm still doing it.'

Teresa was silent for a moment, and Mandy had the impression that she knew much and spoke little.

'Did you see the wheelchair?' Teresa asked, pouring some more coffee.

'Yes, tucked away in the corner.'

'He never uses it if he can help it. And nobody on the "work" side of the house is even supposed to know about it. They all do, of course, but they pretend not to. The door's always locked so that they can't wander in here.'

A locked door, Mandy thought. Somehow that seemed to say everything about Renzo now.

'There was a time,' Teresa continued, 'when this place was like a harem. Do you know how many women chased him?'

'I've got a good idea.'

'Now, he tries to avoid women. He doesn't like them to see him as he is now.'

'It's horrible,' Mandy whispered.

'Yes, it is,' Teresa agreed. 'I'm afraid for him, because if something doesn't happen soon, I think he'll go mad.'

The bell rang from the next room.

'That's him,' Teresa said. 'I must go to him.'

Mandy stayed in the kitchen, trying to work out what she would say when she next saw Renzo.

Today had been a shock, yet she supposed she should have expected it. How unreal now seemed her dreams of instant reconciliation. She shouldn't have turned up without warning. When she next saw him, she would try to repair the damage and start again.

Teresa returned a few moments later, seeming troubled.

'He wants you to go,' she said.

'But I must talk to him again.'

'He says I'm not to let you back in under any circumstances, and he means it. When he's in that mood you can't argue with him. Shall I call you a taxi?'

'No need. My hotel is just in the next street.'

She named it, but Teresa shook her head.

'He won't change his mind. He's as stubborn as granite these days.'

There was nothing for Mandy to do but leave. As she walked away from the house she couldn't resist glancing back, although she knew it was pointless. He wouldn't be looking out to catch a glimpse of her. Renzo had bolted and barred himself from all the world and there was no way in, even for her. The man she'd longed to find was dead after all: as dead as if he'd never lived.

CHAPTER SIX

THE thought of staring at four walls was intolerable so, instead of returning to the hotel, Mandy walked the streets of Milan until she was tired.

Well, what did I expect? she demanded of herself. *I've been a fool, living in a dream world. It's not just that he doesn't know me, it's that he doesn't* want *to know me. I ought to leave, but I can't yet because there's still something he needs to know.*

At last she wandered back to the hotel and put through a call to her flat in England. It was answered by Sue, the friend she'd told Renzo about, long ago, who now lived with her.

'How did it go?' Sue asked.

'Badly. He's a different man. Oh, Sue, I don't know how I'm going to manage this. I thought it would be so simple, and I should have known better. I used to wonder why he'd never tried to find me, but how could he when he didn't know if I was real?'

'Have you told him—anything?'

'No. I have to wait for the right time, only I'm afraid it may never come.'

'Mandy, do you still love him?'

She drew a long breath before saying, 'I don't even know that any more. How can I? I don't know who he is.'

'Danny's just woken up. He learned a new word and he wants to tell you about it.'

'Oh, yes,' Mandy said eagerly. 'Put him on.'

A moment later there was a gurgle on the other end.

'Hello, darling, it's Mummy. I love you.'

'Fish!'

'Is that your new word? You're so clever.'

'Fish, fish, fish!' Danny yelled. 'Mummy, Mummy, fish.'

'Yes, darling,' she said through tears. 'Mummy's a fish. I miss you so much. I'll be home soon, I hope. But Daddy needs me just now. I love you.'

She hung up and dropped her head into her hands, weeping for the child who didn't know his father, and the father who didn't know his child.

* * *

Mandy was awoken next morning by the phone. It was Lucia, the secretary.

'He says you must come back. Right now. Please come quickly. You don't know what he's like when he doesn't get what he wants.'

'I'll be right there.'

Mandy dressed quickly but carefully, managing to look elegant and serious in perfectly cut trousers. When she was sure she was just right, she walked the short distance to his house.

Renzo was waiting for her in the room where she'd last seen him. He was in the wheelchair, but otherwise looked better.

'Thank you for coming so quickly,' he said. 'I forgot my manners yesterday. Please forgive me.'

'Of course. You were unwell.'

'I invited you back because we were trapped together in that avalanche. My memory is patchy but…I do remember you.'

He said the last words with difficulty because they alarmed him. Seeing this woman, a stranger yet oddly familiar, had been a shock, one that he'd tried to cope with by ejecting her. But she wouldn't be ejected. She'd returned in the night, bringing with her a host of impressions that pounded on his brain and demanded entrance.

They had to fight with a million other impressions. His fall had left him with a broken pelvis and severe spinal injuries, and the memory of that savage agony haunted him still.

In the long weeks in hospital he thought perhaps he'd gone mad—hallucinating, his mind filled with many things that did not make sense. Dancers had spun and whirled, a blazing sun set behind the mountains, and a cheeky little cat mysteriously came and went.

He'd left hospital much sooner than the doctors had advised, to take charge of his business, which had been ailing without him. He'd told himself that he had everything under control. The pain was bad but manageable, his employees obeyed him without question, he was feared and respected.

It was only sometimes that he was troubled—in the still of the night, when the pretty cat with sleek black fur and green eyes returned and wandered impudently through his dreams, before vanishing into the shadows.

She had been there last night, teasing and provoking him until he'd awoken, trembling uncontrollably.

There was only one thing for a well-organised man to do: confront the danger, deal with it and neutralise it.

'Won't you sit down?' he said politely, indicating a chair.

He was already filling her cup from the teapot. 'You prefer tea to coffee, I seem to recall. You and Henry.'

'You remember him?' she asked quickly.

'How could anyone forget him?'

'He died.'

'Yes, I know. Also Joan and Peter, for which I blame myself. I should never have let them come up with me. Thank goodness you're all right. I have enough on my conscience.' Before she could reply, he glanced up, saying, 'Here's Teresa with the food. I ordered you a complete English breakfast.'

It was perfect—cornflakes, bacon and eggs, toast. Mandy tucked in, really hungry, but also glad of the chance to think rather than talk. Seeing Renzo yesterday—harsh, ill-tempered, unlike the man she remembered, had been unsettling. Now he was smooth, courteous and at ease, but it was the ease of a man who'd hoisted his defences into place. If anything, she'd preferred him yesterday.

'I was too agitated to ask your name,' he said smoothly. 'I got it from Lucia after you left. I remember—there was a Mandy Jenkins in the hut with me. They found her things there, with mine. We were there, weren't we?'

'For two days.'

'It must have been very uncomfortable. Part

of the hut was missing, I recall. And it was freezing cold.'

'We huddled in blankets, and for food we had to make do with the little that was left in the kitchen.'

'A sad end to a trip that had started so well, except that I think you and I got off on the wrong foot. I annoyed you with some remark I made.'

'You said I looked delicate,' she replied lightly.

'Ah, that was it. But you proved me wrong. You were a much better climber than I expected.'

'Yes, we surprised each other in lots of ways.'

Here was a chance to trigger off the memories of their personal closeness, their jokey, teasing relationship which had been so sweet even while they'd riled each other.

'Well, I must admit—' he started to say, then saw Teresa approaching again. 'Yes, please, Teresa, we'll have some more tea.'

While Teresa removed the pot, Mandy held her breath for what he would say next.

'Where was I?' he said at last. 'Ah, yes, I must admit that everyone on that trip surprised me. That's what comes of taking over someone else's expedition. Pierre judged very badly, and I meant to tell him so when he came to see me in hospital. But he was in such a state that I couldn't. He felt so guilty that he closed his business and vanished.'

'Yes, I heard he'd gone,' she said in a blank voice.

Her disappointment was severe. He remembered her, but only as one of the crowd.

'But why should Pierre feel guilty?' she asked. 'Henry was a bad choice but Pierre couldn't have foreseen his behaviour.'

'That's what I told him.'

'And you shouldn't blame yourself. You were a great leader.'

She was mouthing platitudes, saying anything to keep talking, hoping to find the place where a door could open.

'I remember on the first day out,' she went on desperately, 'Joan slipped and I supported her for a moment. I felt so proud of myself, but actually you were there supporting both of us, as you couldn't resist pointing out to me the following evening.'

'Did I? That was rather rude of me.'

'No, it wasn't rude at all. We were just bickering as usual. It was rather fun, don't you remember?'

Renzo made a wry face. 'Not yet, but I'm sure it will come back soon.'

Mandy felt snubbed. He spoke as an adult patronising a recalcitrant child.

There was silence as Teresa returned with

fresh tea, and it stretched on when she'd departed. Mandy struggled to find words but she seemed to be facing a blank wall.

'We used to have some choice names for each other,' she said.

'I'm sure I never called you names.'

'You used to say I was a little cat— Hey, careful!'

He'd dropped his spoon with a clatter. Mandy retrieved it and realized that he was staring at her. His face had gone very pale.

'I said that?' he asked.

'Once or twice. It was just a joke. It's because of my black hair and green eyes.'

'Anything else?' he asked raggedly.

'You said I was like a feline, insinuating myself wherever I wanted to be. You even said I insinuated myself into your mind and wouldn't go away.' She gave a slight laugh. 'I reminded you that I was always awkward, and you agreed at once.'

'How very brave of me,' he said, trying to match her light-hearted air.

But the effort was too much. The strain he was suppressing broke through.

'Why did you come here?' he asked suddenly. 'Why now, after two years?'

'I thought you were dead, or I'd have come

before. I only found out recently that you were still alive.'

'And you came to see how I was. That's very kind—but why?'

The answer almost burst from her.

Because we were close in heart and mind, as well as body. Because you told me that you loved me just before you were snatched away from me, and I can't forget that, although you've forgotten it as though it never happened. And because we have a child.

But all she said was, 'Surely it's not surprising that I should be concerned? We spent two days in that hut, half starving, freezing, talking, tripping over things in the dark.'

'Ah, yes,' he murmured. 'That sort of thing creates a bond between people, doesn't it?'

'Yes—' she began eagerly.

'And so they become friends.'

She bit back her disappointment. She was becoming good at that.

'Yes,' she said brightly. 'Friends. And friends look out for each other.'

Renzo raised his head to look at her directly and she saw him with new eyes. His features were much the same, if a little older, thinner. But the light behind them was different. Harsh, tense, despairing.

'Thank you,' he said politely. 'It's good to have friends. How did we become separated?'

'You went into the forbidden room—'

'Forbidden—'

'We called it that because the front wall was missing, so we avoided it except when we needed to see outside. I found you there, looking out for a helicopter, and then the ground started to go again. You pushed me to safety, but the floor gave way under you. I know I began screaming, but then I passed out, and the next thing I know I woke up in the hospital.

'They told me afterwards that a helicopter did fly over the hut, and they landed a team to burrow into the snow, just in case. That was how they found me. My friend, Sue—I told you about her—came for me and took me home. She's stayed with me ever since.'

And she was with me while I bore your child.

But the words wouldn't come. Not yet.

'What about you?' she asked. 'You must have been badly hurt.'

'I broke my pelvis, did some damage to my spine,' he said with a shrug.

'And you fool around getting out of that wheelchair when you shouldn't?' she demanded. 'Are you crazy?'

'If I don't walk, I won't recover proper

movement,' he snapped. 'I'm not supposed to live in this thing all the time.'

'But you are supposed to be sensible about getting out of it too often, aren't you? And sensible is one thing you're not.'

His temper flared. '*I'm* not sensible? Look at yourself. You're the crazy woman who insisted on coming with me when I went after Henry. I warned you, but would you be told? Did anyone ever tell you anything? You were trouble from the word *go*.'

She knew a surge of relief at the way anger had freed his mind.

'So you do remember that?'

'Yes, it suddenly came back. I don't know why.'

'Because you lost your temper. That's great.'

'Most people don't enjoy it when I get angry.'

'I'll bet they don't. You terrified that poor man yesterday—'

'That *poor* man tried to cheat me out of a very large sum of money. He thought because my body is damaged my mind was damaged also. He was wrong, as I took great pleasure in proving to him. If he takes it any further I'll make him sorry he was born.'

'And enjoy doing it,' she observed.

'*Yes!*'

There was a hard silence, then he said, 'You must allow a man his few remaining pleasures.'

'I suppose so. It just seems a sad way to enjoy yourself.'

'Most of the other ways are closed off to me. I take what I can. I don't go out among people too much because I hate the way they stare at me.'

'Perhaps they're just friends, sympathising.'

'Some of them. Mostly not. Especially women. I can see them wondering if my skills are the same. They go into a ghastly parody of flirtation and they imagine I don't know what they're thinking—can he, can't he? Shall I put it to the test?'

'No,' she protested in horror. 'You must be wrong about that. Nobody could be so cruel.'

'What do you know about it?' he raged.

'Perhaps they really do find you attractive?'

'I'd have to be very conceited to believe that.'

'Or maybe they're just trying to be nice.'

'Pity, you mean? Show the poor cripple a little mercy, he has so little in his life. *Do you think that's what I want?*' He slammed his hand down on the chair.

The unexpected window onto his suffering left Mandy too shocked to speak. After a moment she managed to say, 'I only meant that you don't really know what people are thinking.'

'Don't tell me what I know. In the past I moved among the kind of women who gave a man marks out of ten. I'm paying for it now. I promise you, I know *exactly* what they're thinking.'

Suddenly he rose, forcing himself out of the chair so fast that he was unsteady and had to grab the furniture. Instinctively, she put out her hand but was repelled by the ferocity in his eyes.

'Don't touch me.'

Mandy backed off, horrified to discover that she was actually afraid of him.

But he relented at once, with a wry look and a placating gesture. 'Ignore me. I get like this sometimes and I take it out on whomever happens to be there.'

Renzo made his way back to the wheelchair. It looked like defeat.

'What were we talking about?' he asked wearily.

'Me, insisting on coming with you after Henry. You think I was just being awkward but I went with you because I thought you might appreciate some support. That was stupid of me. In fact—'

'What is it?' he demanded, seeing her suddenly pale face.

'Nothing, I just thought— Oh, heavens!'

'What is it? Tell me.' He reached out and grasped her hand. 'Tell me!'

'If I hadn't insisted on following you, Joan and Peter wouldn't have come, and they might be alive now. You're right—it was my fault.'

'No, that wasn't what I was saying. I wasn't accusing you of anything.'

'You don't have to—it's true.'

His fingers tightened on her hand with sudden urgency. 'Listen to me. Don't start thinking like that. Hell lies that way.' His voice lowered. 'And, believe me, I know about hell.'

'Yes, you do,' she whispered.

'Once you let the demons into your mind, you can't get rid of them. Don't let them in, Mandy.'

'It's too late,' she said. 'They've been there all the time. Not just Joan and Peter, but you. You saved my life, throwing me to safety. If I'd grabbed you a little faster, I might have stopped you falling away.'

'You couldn't have done that,' he said in the most gentle voice she'd heard him use yet. 'You hit your head on the wall, and that stunned you.'

'I've often thought,' she said slowly, 'what might have happened if you'd just grabbed me and run to the back. We might both have been safe.'

'Or we might both have gone over. There wasn't time. I was desperate to get you to safety, and throwing you in that rather brutal fashion was the quickest way.'

'Or if I'd stayed at the back of the room instead of coming closer to you in that stupid way, you wouldn't have had to save me at all, and you might have had time to save yourself.'

He stopped her with a finger over her mouth, and she saw kindness in his eyes.

'It wasn't your fault. Nothing was your fault.'

'But how do you know if you can't remember?' she dared to ask.

It was a mistake. He drew back.

'I don't know what I remember,' he said. 'Things I thought were real turn out to be figments of my imagination and…the other way round. That's why talking to you is so useful.'

He said the last word deliberately, like a shield being put into place. Her heart sank. And yet she'd been given more than she'd dared hope for.

His face changed again, becoming haggard and racked with a pain that was more than physical.

'Talk to me,' she begged. 'It's been a bad time for me too. We can help each other as nobody else could.'

'Maybe,' he said. 'Or maybe it would be the opposite, for both of us.'

Mandy understood. She might be the one to unlock the demons he was suppressing with iron control, and the resulting catastrophe would destroy him. He was already terrifyingly close to that edge.

'How do you survive?' he whispered.

'I wasn't as badly hurt as you. But you didn't mean that, did you?'

'In here,' he said, indicating his head. 'At night, in the dark.'

'I'm not as alone as you. I have help.'

'Ah, yes, your friend, Sue.'

She drew a deep breath, knowing that the moment had come when she could tell him about Danny, the child of hope who could bring him new life, as he'd done for her.

'It's not just her—'

She stopped, for he'd covered his eyes with his hand.

'Never mind,' he said harshly. 'I didn't mean to ask.'

'But I'll gladly tell you—'

'Another time, perhaps. I need to be alone.'

The moment had gone. There was nothing to do but face it.

'All right, you've had enough. Get some rest.'

Smiling faintly, he nodded. Unable to stop herself, she laid her hand against his face. He might spurn her, but nothing could have stopped her offering him comfort in the hope of breaking through the barrier he'd built around himself.

At first he didn't move, but then he touched her hand, holding it against him. His eyes closed, his whole body shook, and she realized that, incredibly, he was weeping.

Then he pushed her hand away.

'Go,' he said curtly. 'Just go.'

'Shall I come back tomorrow?'

'No…yes…I don't know. I'll call you.'

'I'll be waiting.'

He didn't reply, and her heart broke for him. As she left, she turned to see him sitting in the wheelchair, his back towards her, his body rigid. As she walked away, her hand was still wet with his tears.

Mandy half expected him to call her later that day, but he didn't. Nor the next day.

When she telephoned Sue, her friend was indignant. 'Don't let him treat you like this. March in there and tell him he's got a son and it's time he faced facts.'

'No,' Mandy said at once. 'That would only make him retreat further. He'll only come back if he comes willingly. If not—'

She couldn't make herself finish the sentence. It was too soon to face the possibility of another parting, truly final this time.

But, as the days passed with no word from him, she grew annoyed. Whatever his feelings, he had no right to treat her like a pathetic ex-girlfriend, dumped because she was a bore.

Again and again, her mind played over the end of their last meeting, when anger had made him speak without restraint and his hard face had softened, just for a moment. And then he had wept, and she'd dared to hope that warmth might grow again between them.

But perhaps the fact that she'd seen his tears had been her undoing. After that he'd wanted to get rid of her.

On the third day she rebelled. If he thought she was going to sit here awaiting his pleasure, he was badly mistaken. She was, after all, in Milan, a city so famous for fashion that it had given the world the word *milliner*. She spent a fascinating afternoon studying the expensive shops, ended in a restaurant and took a taxi back to the hotel.

'*Signorina,*' said the receptionist as soon as she entered, 'a gentleman has left many messages for you to call him back.'

The relief was overwhelming. It had come right at last, as she had surely known it would. Taking the paper he held out, she hurried up to her room and dialled the number she saw written there.

'*Pronto!*' The voice that answered was not Renzo's.

'This is the Signorina Amanda Jenkins,' she said hesitantly.

'*Signorina,* thank you so much for calling back. My name is Eugenio Ferrini. I understand that you are a researcher of the highest calibre.'

She sat down abruptly on the bed. It wasn't Renzo. He still hadn't called her.

Mandy made some reply, and the smooth voice at the other end explained that he was embarking on a book for which he would need some research done in England, and she had been recommended to him.

'Why me?' she asked, dazed.

'Your name is better known than you think. My wife and I would be so glad if you would join us for dinner tomorrow evening. I can show you my papers and we can discuss the work you can do for me.'

'Thank you, I should love to,' she said, making a note of his address.

At least this way her trip would not be wasted, she thought angrily.

His house was close to the Via Montenapoleone, the fashionable street where she'd walked that very afternoon, and therefore the most expensive part of town. If the Ferrinis lived there, she had better take a lot of trouble about her appearance.

By next morning there was still no call from Renzo and she set out on a shopping trip in a mood of determination. First Gucci, then Armani, then Louis Vuitton, then a dozen others, until she had settled on a simple dress of dark green that echoed her eyes, set off with tiny earrings that were a convincing imitation of gold, and shoes with suicidally high heels that did wonders for her ankles and legs.

Then it was the beauty parlour for a session that left her skin dazzling and her hair teased into a curvy confection, disdaining the slight severity of her usual style. When she'd returned to the hotel and donned her new clothes she knew herself to be fit for the most glamorous party.

A limousine called at exactly seven o'clock and conveyed her the short distance to the Ferrini villa, which looked as if it had been built several hundred years earlier by an inspired architect.

Lights poured from the building and her host was already at the door on the top of the steps, smiling in welcome.

'*Dottoressa*, how kind of you to come at such short notice.'

She was astonished. Her college degrees

entitled her to be addressed as 'Doctor' but it was still surprising that Ferrini had known it. How much did he know about her, and who had told him?

He was a small, thin man with white hair, a lean face and a brilliant smile. He introduced his family, then took her inside, where she received a shock. She'd expected a small gathering, but there were at least a hundred people there, enjoying pre-dinner drinks.

Ferrini introduced her as an honoured guest, repeating *Dottoressa* several times, so that they should all appreciate that a person of distinction had come among them. And Mandy soon realized that they were genuinely impressed. They were Italians, with a respect not only for learning but for the indefinable quality known as *bella figura*. It was something she had noticed in Renzo—style, assurance. Now she sensed that her fellow guests could see it in her, and her confidence flowered.

The others were dressed in the costliest of jewels, the most elegant of clothes, but it was Mandy who stood out, perhaps because she had chosen a simple look. Or perhaps because she was stunning. The men opened their eyes wider at the sight of her, and many of them jostled to get close and offer her wine.

Only one man did neither. Like the others, he watched the new arrival carefully, but only from the shelter of a large bookcase, to see without being seen, for he feared prying eyes.

If they could observe him now they would rake him over, fascinated by the longing which he tried to hide but feared he couldn't. Worst of all, *she* might guess the truth.

He'd seen a difference in her from the start. Her face was no longer the cheeky imp he'd known before, but older, thinner, marked by sadness, yet no less entrancing. It added one more confusion to those that already swamped him, and her appearance tonight— chic, beautiful—only compounded his bewilderment.

And she knew she was beautiful. Oh, how she knew it!

Suddenly he was back in that other time, when she'd forced him to watch her with another man, dancing as though they were one, moving sinuously, provocatively, teasing, taunting him, daring him to take action.

And he hadn't dared, because what he'd wanted to do was toss her over his shoulder, carry her to bed and make love until they were both dizzy.

Which, might, just possibly, have caused a scandal.

Now, she was doing it again, flickering through the lights, vanishing, reappearing, luring him on yet, with every movement, every turn of her head, proclaiming herself queen of her surroundings and far, far out of his reach.

CHAPTER SEVEN

'SHALL we go through to dinner now?' Ferrini asked Mandy.

At once his two grown sons stepped forward, inviting her to take the arm of one or both of them.

'Be off,' their father commanded, laughing and crooking his own arm. 'Age has its privileges.'

'But you don't need to claim privilege,' Mandy said lightly. 'You are the one I would have chosen.'

This raised a cheer and a smattering of applause, led by Ferrini's much entertained wife. Mandy accepted his arm, glancing triumphantly around at her audience. Then she froze with shock.

Just for a moment she thought she'd seen Renzo, standing in the far corner of the room, watching her intently. But surely it was her imagination. One blink and he was gone.

'Are you all right?' Ferrini asked gallantly.

'Perfectly,' she said brightly. 'Except that I'm famished, and longing for this splendid meal.'

'Then let us depart on the instant.'

Signora Ferrini prided herself on having the best cook in Milan, and it showed. With every course, several dishes were on offer—saffron-coloured Risotto alla Milanese, Frito Misto, a mixed fry of seafoods and meat, Osso Buco, veal shank garnished with parsley, garlic and lemon rind, followed by Lombardy apple fritters and paradise cake.

While eating she took the chance to glance along the table, seeking the face that she might—or might not—have seen earlier. But it was some distance and the people at the far end were indistinct.

I've got to stop this, she told herself. *Of course he can't be here. He's not well enough.*

Then she saw him, sitting at the far end, deep in conversation with a vivacious young woman who was clearly straining every nerve to hold his attention. He wore a black dinner jacket and bow tie, just as he had the night he'd leapt into her room, certain of his right to do as he pleased whether it was to seduce one woman or comically throw himself on the mercies of another.

It was a shock to see that he could still look

like the old Renzo—handsome, confident, basking in female adoration.

So that was why she'd been ignored, Mandy thought indignantly. Renzo had learned all he wanted to from her, decided it didn't interest him and turned away, leaving her sitting, waiting in the hotel like an idiot. No doubt he thought that by now she'd have given up and left Milan. The last thing he'd expected was to see her here, which was why he'd been trying to escape her notice.

Angrily, she focused on her host and asked about the work he wanted her to do. He explained that he was writing a history of his family, whose activities over the generations had been colourful.

'We have long had a connection with England. Many Ferrini wives have come from there, some from notable political families, and it is this that I would like you to work on.'

'Pooh, politics!' said the young man on her other side.

Turning, Mandy saw Luigi, Ferrini's younger son, in his early twenties and one of the most dazzlingly handsome young men she had ever met. His eyes were dark and lustrous, gazing into hers with a fervour that made her want to laugh.

'*Dottoressa*,' he said, taking her hand, 'our history contains many great love stories that are far more important than politics. The Ferrini men have gone out and conquered.' He carried her hand to his lips. 'I'm sure you understand me.'

'I understand you perfectly,' she said with meaning.

'Behave yourself, Luigi,' Ferrini commanded. 'You will embarrass our guest.'

'Not at all,' Mandy said lightly, recovering her hand. 'I'm very good at coping with over eager little boys.'

This caused a general laugh. Luigi smote his forehead.

'She calls me a little boy. *Dottoressa*, this will never do. I must have my revenge.'

'Perhaps I will also take mine,' she murmured.

'Is that a promise?'

'No,' she said, smiling provocatively. 'It's a threat.'

This caused another laugh. Under the cover of looking around her, Mandy managed to dart a quick glance down the table. She might as well not have bothered. Renzo was totally absorbed in his lovely companion. There was nothing to suggest that he'd seen what was going on at the other end.

The meal was coming to an end. People

split into groups, drifting out into the beautiful gardens.

'Perhaps we could now go into the library,' Ferrini said.

'Let us all go,' Luigi added, drawing Mandy's hand through his arm.

Together, the three of them headed out of the dining room, Luigi talking non-stop, both to her and the other guests as he passed them.

'Of course we all think our own family is interesting, but ours has produced more scoundrels than most—Elena, how lovely to see you again—plus a few who can claim royal blood—unofficially. Of course that's shocking but—ah, my friend, Renzo, I was wondering where you were. Do you know Signorina Jenkins?'

'I have that pleasure,' Renzo said, rising to his feet and nodding politely at Mandy. 'Good evening, *Dottoressa*. I trust you're enjoying yourself.'

'More than I would have believed possible,' she replied. 'I can't tell you how glad I am that I came.' She added significantly, 'I'm learning so much.'

It would have been a pleasure to see him discomfited, but his face was blank as he gave another brief nod before Luigi swept her away.

A man standing just behind Renzo gave an envious sigh.

'So Luigi's in love again, but you can't blame him this time. She's a pearl among women, don't you think?' Receiving no answer, he peered closer. 'Renzo, are you with us?'

'Forgive me,' Renzo said with an effort. 'What were you saying?'

'I asked what you thought of Luigi's latest little playmate.' His voice trailed off at the murderous look he found turned on him.

'Be silent if you know what's good for you,' Renzo said softly. 'Do you understand me?'

'Yes…yes…no offence meant… I only…'

'Get out of my sight.'

The man backed away, exchanging a glance with the pretty young woman beside Renzo, who'd been determinedly flirting with him. Now she gave a shrug and a resigned sigh. Another hope gone.

Mandy's hosts escorted her across the marble hall to a pair of ornate double doors, which Ferrini pulled open to reveal a huge old-fashioned library with books going up to the ceiling. It also boasted a top-of-the-range computer, but the predominant impression was of another century. She was charmed.

She was also slightly puzzled when she examined papers and heard Ferrini's detailed description of what he wanted her to do. The notes were extensive and the ground seemed to have been well covered already. But the fee he was offering was considerable, and she had no other work in prospect.

At last the door opened to reveal Ferrini's elder son.

'Papa, Signor Marucci wants to speak to you urgently—'

Her host said something very impolite about Signor Marucci.

'Don't worry,' Luigi said. 'I'll look after the *Dottoressa*. There are many things you haven't told her.'

'Can you endure this bad character?' Ferrini asked her, grinning.

'He doesn't frighten me,' Mandy said. She waited until the other two had left, then said firmly to Luigi, 'Shall we get to work?'

She had to admit that when he got talking he was serious and interesting, giving her insights that his father had overlooked. But he also gazed at her like a lovesick puppy, making it hard for her to keep a straight face.

'I think we should join the others now,' she said.

'Haven't I earned a reward?' he asked plaintively.

'You've certainly earned my thanks.'

'Is that all? Not one little kiss?' He began to advance on her.

'Listen to me, Luigi. You're a very nice person, but I'm several years older than you and I don't play games with children.'

'I'm not a child. I'll show you.'

He managed to get an arm around her waist but she fended him off with a hand pressed firmly against his chest.

'I'm warning you, Luigi—'

'But now I simply must kiss you,' he said winsomely. 'It's a matter of honour.'

In the brief tussle that followed he succeeded in planting the tiniest possible peck on her cheek before she managed to get free and head for the door. Then she froze.

Renzo was standing there.

'Our host asked me to fetch you,' he said tonelessly. 'There's going to be dancing.'

'Good,' she said a little breathlessly, 'I enjoy dancing.'

'Yes, I remember.'

'Splendid,' Luigi declared, unabashed. 'Now I can dance with you.'

But now the game had palled.

'I don't think so,' she said. 'You have other guests. I mustn't monopolise you.'

He tried to get close again, but Renzo forestalled him, extending his arm for Mandy to take.

'Well, don't let Renzo monopolise *you*,' Luigi said blithely. 'He won't dance with you. He can't. He's a dead man these days.'

Mandy heard someone draw a sharp breath. It might have been Renzo or herself. She couldn't be sure because a red mist had descended on her.

'What a rotten thing to say!' she flashed. 'You should be ashamed of yourself.'

'All right,' he said, backing away. 'Don't eat me. I'm just warning you that he's not the man he was.'

'He's still ten times the man you are,' she raged. 'Let me go, Renzo.'

He'd settled his arms around her tightly enough to withstand her struggles.

'*Let me go.*'

'Hush,' he said, holding on. 'You can't murder him in his own house. It wouldn't be polite. Luigi, clear off or, I swear, I'll set her on you.'

Luigi fled.

When he was out of sight, she stood for a moment, breathing hard, shattered by her own reaction. She'd thought she was in command until Luigi had insulted Renzo. Now she was in a blazing temper, and turned it on him for lack of any other target.

'Why did you do that?' she blazed. 'Did you hear what he said about you?'

He nodded. 'I heard what you said too. There was a time when you'd have gone to the stake rather than pay me a compliment.'

'I wasn't complimenting you,' she said quickly. 'I just said it to put him down.'

'Ah, yes, I should have realized that.'

'I was annoyed at his callousness. Didn't it make you angry when he said you were a—' She stopped, unable to say it.

'A dead man?' Renzo finished for her. 'Why shouldn't he say it? It's true. I've been a dead man for two years, but perhaps— Who knows?'

The stab of pleasure this gave her made her doubly conscious that he was still holding her firmly against him. His grip was strong, not at all like an invalid, and the warmth from his body seemed to envelop her.

'Will you please let me go?' she asked in a shaking voice.

'I don't think I should. You're not a safe person to be on the loose. You never were. The first time we met, you threatened to thump me.'

'No, our meeting in the office wasn't the first meeting. There was one before that.'

He nodded. 'Yes, there was. I behaved very badly, didn't I?'

'Shockingly.'

'And you were wearing that towel robe that kept falling open.'

'I don't remember,' she said, trying to dismiss the pictures that flashed through her brain.

'Neither did I for a long time, but I've remembered now.' His smile came from the old days and told her that his memory contained every detail of that night. To her intense annoyance, she found that she was blushing.

'Nothing to say?' he asked wryly. 'That's not like you. You were always waiting to catch me out.'

'I liked my fun,' she said defiantly.

'Not that night. We could have had fun together—'

'I'd barely met you.'

'You'd barely met Luigi tonight but it didn't stop you egging him on.'

'I didn't— How dare—' She was speechless.

'Let's go out into the garden, where we can have a drink and talk.'

Renzo began to lead her out of the house, still

his prisoner, and now she found that the desire to escape had mysteriously faded.

The sound of music reached them from the garden and they wandered out to find it lit with fairy lights. There was a small orchestra and a patio where couples were dancing. Beyond it, people were wandering among the fountains, drinking champagne, talking softly.

'Let's dance,' he said, adjusting his hold so that she was completely in his arms.

'Can you dance?'

He gave her a wry smile. 'That bit of me is still alive.'

He danced slowly, but seemingly without difficulty, which puzzled her. Only recently he'd been in such pain that he'd needed a wheelchair. Now it was hard to tell that there was anything wrong with him.

One thing was clear to her. He'd been wrong that time when he'd said women stared at him only out of cruel calculation. They were staring at him now, and their expressions were the same ones she'd seen in the Alps: curiosity, desire, anticipation. But no pity.

With her high heels she could almost look him in the eye, something he seemed to appreciate, for he held her gaze steadily and his mouth was dangerously close.

She tried to remember that she was angry with him for ignoring her for days, but the pleasure of his presence had made everything else retreat into the distance. He'd always had that effect and it was as annoying now as it had been then. She wanted to tell him to stop his nonsense. She wanted to kick his shins—very gently. She wanted to kiss him.

'I'm suspicious of you,' she said at last.

'No change there, then,' he murmured, so that she felt his breath softly touching her face.

'I mean, I want to know what's brought about this miracle recovery.'

'I'm a genius, hadn't you heard?'

'Yes, you've told me. I never believed it, then or now.'

'That's what I was afraid of.' He sighed.

'Will you be serious? Have you done something stupid? Yes, of course you have. You've got no sense.'

'True. There's a lot going through my head just now, but none of it's sensible.'

'Does it matter?' She chuckled. 'Common sense is for wimps.'

'I couldn't agree more.'

'If I were being really sensible, I'd wonder at the coincidence of us both turning up here tonight.' When he didn't reply, she cocked her head on one side and challenged him. 'It's not an accident, is it?'

He eyed her warily. 'What do you think?'

'I think you're the most devious, unscrupulous… If I really told you what I thought of you, we'd be here all night. You set it up, didn't you?'

'I admit nothing.'

'You don't have to. If ever a man appeared guilty—'

'No, no, you misunderstand,' he said with a grin. 'That isn't guilt. It's conceit at getting my own way.'

'Of course it is.'

At that moment Ferrini danced by. He was amazed at the sight of Mandy.

'*Mio dio!* I meant to send someone to fetch you and I completely forgot. Never mind. Here you are.'

He danced away. Mandy stared indignantly at Renzo, who was looking sheepish.

'You told me he sent you to fetch me,' she accused.

'Did I? I forget.'

'You're a rotten liar.'

'No, actually, I'm a very good liar,' he said outrageously. 'I can produce a hundred witnesses to testify to my skill at being most con-

vincing when I'm most dishonest. Look, you
were on your own with Luigi. You might have
needed help.'

'You were protecting me?'

'Didn't you protect me back there?'

That silenced her just for a moment, until
she recovered enough to say, 'Don't get all
offended and full of male pride.'

'Oddly enough, I wasn't,' he said softly. 'I
just never thought of you taking up the cudgels
on my behalf.'

'I don't like people having a go at you,' she
muttered.

'You mean, you reserve that privilege for
yourself?'

'Something like that. Anyway, we're even
now. Though why you thought I needed help to
deal with that silly boy, I don't know.'

'I know what he can be like.'

'Like you at the same age,' she ventured.

'I was much worse,' he said with a grin.

'Why do I find that so easy to believe?' she
asked of the air.

'Because you know me better than I know
myself, which is alarming. I keep wondering,
What did I do that she knows and I don't?'

She gave him an impish smile which came
and went in the fairy lights.

'If you're hoping I'm going to tell you,' she murmured, 'think again.'

'Little cat. Don't torment me—tell me.'

'No. There are some things a man must remember for himself, or they weren't important.'

'And it was important, wasn't it, Mandy?'

'Oh, yes.'

'Tell me.'

'Be patient. It'll come to you.'

'And if it doesn't?'

'Then I'll just have to go away.'

His arms tightened. 'I won't let you. I'll keep you prisoner.'

'You won't find that easy. I'll escape.'

He leaned down so that his mouth was close to hers. 'Give me a clue.'

'Let's think—what do you *want* to do, right this minute?'

His eyes gleamed, but he seemed puzzled, as well.

'Mandy—are you telling me—it wasn't just my imagination?'

She lifted her head a little and laid her lips against his. 'Remember,' she whispered.

The next moment she'd slid free of him and glided away. Before he could follow her, she was in the arms of another partner.

Renzo went to sit at the edge of the patio, where he could watch her. His mind was reeling with the impressions chasing through it. Had he understood her properly? Would any woman tease about such a thing if it wasn't true? Did he dare to believe her?

A dead man, Luigi had said. But not any more. Even the thought of making love to her was bringing life back to a body resigned to a half existence. It was strange and thrilling in a way he'd thought never to experience again. And his pretty little cat had done it with the merest flick of her tail.

Now the sight of her dancing with other men was as electrifying as it had been the first time. Did she know that? Of course she did.

She glided past, giving him a challenging look that he couldn't mistake. He returned it in full measure, then moved determinedly among the dancers to claim her.

'Hey,' protested her partner. 'You can't do that.'

'Watch me,' Renzo said simply.

'Don't tangle with him,' Mandy advised the young man. 'He knows what he wants.'

As she said it she smiled at Renzo in a way that made him grasp her firmly and swing her away.

'You never said a truer word,' he told her.

'And what I want now is to know where you're leading me.'

She stopped, giving him the same look as a few minutes before, full of promise, daring, provocation.

'All right,' she said, taking his hand. 'Let's find out together.'

She moved him away, keeping hold of him, making him her prisoner as he'd threatened to make her his. But no prisoner had ever been more content. She could sense that, just as she could sense the jealous stares of the other women as they passed. They knew she'd secured the most desirable man in the place. They knew where she was taking him, and what they were going to do. And every one of them was burning with envy.

She had never enjoyed anything more.

Ferrini appeared, laughing, understanding.

'My car will take you home,' he said. 'Look after him, *signorina*. He very much needs it.'

'I know he does.'

The car was ready to take them on the short journey. She fell into the back and reached for him, kissing him eagerly.

'I'm leading you there,' she whispered, 'and here, if that's where you want to go.'

'Mmm,' he said.

'Renzo?' she said as a disturbing dread rose

in her. '*Renzo?* Oh, no, I don't believe this. It can't be happening.'

But it was happening. Renzo's eyes were closed and his head slumped forward.

'*Are you daring to fall asleep?*' she demanded, outraged.

'No,' he said, hastily opening his eyes.

But they closed again at once. He was dead to the world.

CHAPTER EIGHT

When they reached the house, Renzo was just about able to walk inside.

Teresa appeared immediately, looking relieved when she saw him.

'All right, stop fussing,' he said mildly.

'I'll stop fussing when you're safely in bed.'

'Can you manage the stairs?' Mandy asked.

Luckily there was no need. A lift had been installed to take him to his bedroom, one floor up. He leaned against the wall, eyes closed, while Mandy regarded him with outrage. Her whole body was singing with the excitement only he could bring her, and now he couldn't bring matters to a conclusion. She could happily have wrung his neck.

When they reached his room, he fell on the bed with a sigh, and was out like a light.

'Goodnight,' she said stormily. *'Goodnight!'*

Teresa was waiting for her, beckoning Mandy into the room opposite Renzo's.

'It's late,' she said. 'You stay here tonight. He needs you.'

Mandy smiled. Teresa was making a takeover bid. She even had a snack ready and waiting, with English tea, perfectly made.

'This is delicious,' Mandy said.

Suddenly Teresa's loving exasperation exploded. 'I warned him, but would he be told? Those pills are very strong and he's supposed to be careful how many he takes.'

'Pills?'

'Before he left tonight he took three times the dose of painkiller that he's supposed to take.'

'Three times?' Mandy echoed, aghast. 'No wonder he passed out. Should we send for the doctor?'

'No, he's done it before and he wakes up eventually, but it's still dangerous.'

'But why do it tonight?'

'He said he had to be at his best.'

'Yes, in front of all those people—'

'That's not the reason and I think you know it.'

She looked at Mandy. Mandy looked away first.

'I don't know…what I know,' she said reluctantly.

'Now you sound like him,' Teresa observed. 'You're just like each other.'

'Yes, I think we are,' Mandy said with a little smile. She ate a cake slowly before saying, 'You've been with him all his life, haven't you?'

'Most of it. Gina, his mother, couldn't cope, so they employed me.'

'She couldn't cope with one child? Did she have a job, as well?'

'No, she was a lazy cow, thought life revolved around her. When things got difficult she left. You said he told you about that?'

'Just that he came home and found her gone.'

'I'll never forget that day. He'd done a picture of her at school and he wanted to show her. He went all over the house searching, but she wasn't there. She'd left a note for his father, but there was nothing for him. He cried for three days.'

'How could any woman do that to a little boy?' Mandy asked, horrified. 'Didn't she love him at all?'

'I don't think so,' Teresa said reflectively. 'It sometimes happens that a woman can't love one of her children, although she loves the others. She married very young and had him when she was only sixteen. I think she blamed him for the loss of her youth.

'When she'd gone to live with her new man,

she didn't even like Renzo visiting her. There were always excuses. Once he was supposed to be going on holiday with her and her new family, but on the very morning she rang up to say it wasn't "convenient".

'He was twelve years old by then, and I'll never forget his face when he heard. I thought he'd cry, but he didn't. He just turned a ghastly pale colour, then his eyes went dead.

'I was so angry that I went to see Gina and gave her a piece of my mind, but she just said she'd send him a holiday present.'

'And I'll bet she didn't,' Mandy said angrily.

'Oh, yes, she did, but it would have been better if she hadn't. It was a big parcel that looked exciting. He tore the wrapping off, so eager and happy because she'd actually remembered him.'

'What was inside?'

'A photograph. A *family* photograph. It showed Gina and her new husband with their children. She'd written on it, "Love from Mamma" but all Renzo saw was that she loved those children as she'd never loved him.'

'But how could she do anything so cruel?' Mandy exploded.

'Because she's selfish and stupid,' Teresa snapped contemptuously. 'It wouldn't cross her mind to think how an abandoned child would feel at the sight of her with the children who'd replaced him.'

Mandy dropped her head into her hands, anguished for the pain of the rejected child, and the man he'd become.

'After that he seemed to toughen up inside. I suppose he needed to. It was the only way to cope. But I was sorry too, because he changed, began to protect himself.

'He threw himself into school, succeeded at everything, especially athletics. When he was old enough to go away alone, he joined expeditions in the mountains—skiing, climbing, bobsleigh. He won a host of trophies. Look at this.'

Teresa went to a cupboard by her bed, drew out a large album and laid it before Mandy. Leafing through it, she saw again the Renzo she'd known two years before, beaming with victory, a triumphant young hero, usually with a female companion.

'That looks familiar,' she said. 'The first time I met him—'

She described the night Renzo had burst into her room, escaping an indignant husband, and Teresa roared with laughter.

'That's him,' she said. 'Things like that were always happening, but it wasn't his fault. He was so handsome and delightful. All the girls loved him.'

'Did he love them?'

'Not really. He believed that women would always betray men. I think he was infatuated once or twice, but then he always ended it quickly. He was nice about it, let them down gently, but it was final. His barriers were well in place.'

'Barriers,' Mandy said thoughtfully. 'When I knew him first I would never have thought of that in connection with him. He seemed so open to life, to people.'

'But that *is* the barrier,' Teresa said. 'Nobody can get past it to know what he really thinks and feels.'

I did, Mandy thought wistfully. *But only when he thought he was dying.*

'The other side of him was always there,' Teresa continued. 'Angry, hard, wary of people and feelings, but in the beginning it was only now and then. It's the side he used in the business.

'He used his reputation as a winner to get started, then he built it up and made a fortune by being tough. His chief competitor was Enrico Tillani, but he was losing business to Renzo. Finally Renzo bought him out, and after that he was top of the heap.

'Then he'd go out socializing and you'd see

the other man, the one who could charm the birds off the trees.'

'He used to drive me mad with the way he seemed to assume that life—and women—were all his for the taking,' Mandy said. 'But when we were trapped in the hut he was like another man, a man with a real heart. Now all that's gone. I guess he's still protecting himself.'

'If you understand that, then you're the one he needs.'

Mandy glanced through a few more pages of the book before closing it. Teresa immediately replaced it in the cupboard.

'Don't tell him you've seen that,' she said. 'He told me to destroy it, said he never wanted to see or think about it again.'

'What about his mother? How did she react to his accident?'

'She sent him a card,' Teresa said contemptuously. 'She said Australia was too far to come. A card! He just grunted and put it aside.'

Mandy said a rude word.

'That's how I feel about her,' Teresa agreed. 'Here, have a look at this.'

She brought another book from the cupboard. This one was full of family pictures.

'That's her,' Teresa said scornfully, pointing to a photograph of a young woman of about twenty. She had a beautiful but willful face, and a hint of arrogance in the way she held her head.

Spoilt rotten, Mandy thought as she leafed through the rest of the book. Suddenly she stopped.

'What's this?' she asked, pointing to a large picture.

It showed Gina with an older man. The toddler Renzo was there too, but not in his mother's arms. It was the man who held him and watched him with eyes beaming with love and pride.

'That's Bruno, Gina's father. He adored that little boy and he never forgave Gina for what she did to him.'

Receiving no answer, she peered curiously at Mandy. 'Why, what is it?'

'I was just…looking at him, the grandfather…' Mandy said slowly.

'He is a lovely man.' Teresa sighed. 'Generous and sweet-natured, and he really loved Renzo. He had him to stay over as often as he could, and I reckon he gave him all the love he ever knew, for years.

'He never took to Gina's new family. She tried to make him, because he's rich and she had her eye an inheritance. But it was always Renzo, with him.

'He's dying now, and cannot leave hospital.

Renzo goes to see him and talk to him, although I'm not sure how much Bruno understands.'

Mandy looked more closely at the photograph, feeling a swell of joy and relief. For she had seen those happy, laughing features before, on the face of her little son.

Teresa had lent her a nightdress, a vast flannel creation in pink, covered in dancing mushrooms. She slept for a few hours, awaking in the dawn and creeping out into the corridor to listen at Renzo's door, from behind which came muttered curses. She opened it a crack and saw him sitting on the edge of the bed, still dressed.

'Is the Sleeping Beauty awake now?' she asked.

'Grr!'

She came inside and sat beside him, affording him a full view of her attire.

'What—' he demanded, aghast.

'It's Teresa's. I didn't have anything of my own.'

He began to undo his shirt buttons, then stopped, looked at her again and covered his eyes.

'Oh, stop it,' she said, laughing. 'Here, let me help you.'

The last time she'd undressed him it had been in the dark, with love and passion, and he'd undressed her in the same way. Would this touch awaken any memory in the darkened places of his mind?

But the mood was wrong. Nobody could be passionate wearing dancing mushrooms.

And all thoughts of seduction were driven away by the sight of him when they had eased his shirt off together and she saw his scars. For a moment she had to look away to hide the tears.

'It's not too bad,' he said. 'The doctors did a good job and they've healed well. I just look a bit different. It's no big deal.'

He began working on his trousers, and she pulled them off for him. When he was down to his underpants she helped him into bed, pulling the duvet up over him. He was still very sleepy.

'Overdosing on medicine,' she chided him. 'You were supposed to be taking it easy, recovering.'

'I've worked on that these last few days, trying to be in good shape for last night.'

'Because you'd plotted with Eugenio that he would invite me? That's where he got all that *Dottoressa* stuff from.'

'Think what you will of me, the worst is probably all true. Ferrini is an old friend. When I asked him to help me, he agreed at once.'

'But you didn't have to arrange a "chance" meeting. Just call me. Why do it this way?'

Renzo hesitated before saying with difficulty, 'When you first appeared the other day, I was confused. I asked you back the next day because I thought I could handle it, but I couldn't. So I told you to go. I wanted to see you again, but from a distance, so that I could watch without being seen. Yes, that's reprehensible and if you want to call me names, I won't argue.'

'No names, I promise. But wouldn't it have been better for me to come here so that we could talk?'

'I didn't want to talk, just look at you and try to work out if you're the same person who goes through my head in the night.'

'And am I?'

'I think so. Tonight I was almost on the edge of finding out, but I made a mess of everything.'

'It's not your fault you need painkillers. There'll be other times. Do I go through your head often?'

'You come and go, and I'm never sure—' He floundered for a moment, then gave a helpless shrug. 'I'm never sure of anything, these days; just that I can often see someone out of the corner of my eye, but when I turn she vanishes around the corner—if she really existed at all.'

'She does,' Mandy assured him. 'She's real—*I'm* real.'

'But which you? You change all the time.'

'Perhaps I'm waiting for you to say which one of me you prefer.'

'Perhaps I'm waiting for you to be the same person twice, so that I can tell.'

'Do I change so much in your mind?' she asked.

'All the time. But then you always did. When we were in the mountains, one moment you'd be sticking your claws into me, the next you'd say something that made me feel as if our minds were one. I've never had that feeling with anyone else. That ought to make it easier, but it doesn't.' He gave a grunt of mirthless laughter. 'I'm a real headcase.'

'It's probably something to do with all those operations you had,' she mused. 'Too many anaesthetics, close together, scramble your brains.'

'And they stay scrambled,' he said wryly. 'The odd thing is that the further back I go, the clearer my memory becomes. The night we met, that robe you were wearing—you were so beautiful I actually forgot about the woman I was supposed to be making love to.'

'You mean, the one with the outraged husband? One of many, I'll bet.'

He gave a faint smile. 'Yes, I was a bit that way, in those days.'

He said 'in those days' as though describing another universe, and again she had to suppress her emotion. How often in the past had he maddened her? And what wouldn't she give to have him like that again now?

'We were three floors up, but you came leaping over those railings as though it was nothing,' she reminded him.

'Like Douglas Fairbanks, you said. When I got back to my hotel that night, I went online and checked him out. You were right, I was always a show-off. I never impressed you, though, did I?'

'Don't put yourself down. If you were just a show-off, you wouldn't have got under my skin so much. But there were times when it was good. Do you remember that night we talked about freedom?'

'Yes, I do. I'd have liked to talk to you for hours because—'

He stopped as though the next words were difficult, and Mandy held her breath.

'Because I felt I could trust you,' Renzo finished.

She was disappointed, but only for a moment. Trust was a step forward.

'I'm surprised you liked talking to me,' she said lightly, 'since you say I kept digging my claws in.'

'You were always interesting. I never knew where the next attack was going to come from. Mind you, the first night you said something unforgivable. *Ham* actor, indeed!'

'Yes, I really hit home with that one, didn't I?'

He managed a laugh, then immediately winced and wished he hadn't.

'You're feeling bad,' Mandy said. 'Can I get you something?'

'Thanks. My pills are over there.'

'After all you've had—'

'They've worn off, believe me.'

She fetched the pills and poured water from a carafe beside the bed. Renzo took them thankfully, sitting up to do so and moving his shoulders cautiously.

'My spine seems to have a life of its own,' he said. 'The doctors put it right and then it thinks of something else.'

'Perhaps you need Dr Renzo's All Purpose Linctus? I can really recommend it.'

'I must admit there wasn't much in that stuff. I had other motives—disgraceful ones.'

He gave her a cautious glance to see how she was affected by this confession, but she only smiled, saying, 'So it was just the massage that made me feel so much better?'

'I guess it was.'

After a moment she said hesitantly, 'Then perhaps you should let me return the favour—unless you think I might do some damage.'

'You won't do me any damage,' he said quietly. 'I told you I trusted you, and I do—with my life.'

'Lie down.'

When he was face down on the bed, she could see the marks more clearly. As he'd said, they were healed now, and the rest of him looked as strong and well developed as before. But the savage scars told their story of pain and suffering that would always be with him.

Mandy closed her eyes for a moment, struggling to keep her anguished feelings to herself. She had lain with him in the secret darkness, shared with him the knowledge of approaching death, and given him her heart in exchange for his. Now he'd come to this.

'I hope I'm not hurting you,' she said, beginning to rub her hands gently over his back.

'No, don't stop.'

She drew a sharp breath. She'd thought she had command of herself, but these words, an echo of the night they had made love, transfixed her. She had touched him then, so tenderly and passionately that he had cried out for more.

Last night they'd come close to finding each other again, and only bad luck had got in the way. But they had taken a step forward and there would be other times. For the moment all he asked of her was friendship and comfort.

For now she would give them to him, but some day soon the moment would come again. On that she was determined.

Patience, she told herself. But it was hard to be patient when she thought of Danny, the little boy waiting for her at home, who might do so much for his father, and the father who might do so much for him.

She fell into a rhythm, massaging back and forth, while Renzo lay silent, relaxing under her hands until at last his eyes closed.

'How does that feel?' she asked.

When there was no reply she looked at him more closely and saw that he was asleep again, frowning slightly. Slowly, she reached out a tentative hand and laid it against his cheek. He didn't move, but it seemed to her that the frown faded. Holding her breath, she let her fingers drift to his hair, brushing it back from his brow.

She should leave now, but she couldn't make herself do it. Holding her breath, she leaned down and laid her lips against his cheek. He didn't move but she was sure she sensed him relax, grow content. Or perhaps she'd only imagined it from the depths of her longing.

If only he would turn over, open his eyes, smile and welcome her into his arms. But he didn't move. If anything, he seemed more deeply asleep.

Gently, she drew the duvet up over his shoulders, turned out the bedside lamp and backed out of the room.

In some far corner of his consciousness Renzo heard the soft closing of the door, but it didn't disturb the sensuous dream in which he was drifting. Hands caressed him softly and a voice from long ago whispered, 'I love you.'

'Who are you?' he begged. 'Let me see your face.'

'You don't need to see my face,' she whispered. 'You know me.'

But he didn't know her. He reached out, seeking vainly for something that would clear the clouds that had shrouded his mind for the last two years.

But she was gone again, as she always was.

Mandy slept later than she'd meant to, and when she went downstairs Ferrini was already there with Renzo. He rose to greet her, beaming

'Your hotel told me you hadn't returned last night, so I came here. I know that your arrival will be the best thing for my friend Renzo, as it will be for me.'

'Signor Ferrini, I must tell you that I know why you invited me last night. Renzo asked you to.'

'I don't deny it, but I still need your professional help. All we have to do is discuss money. Renzo says that you can leave the hotel and live here—'

'So it's all settled,' Renzo said, regarding her with a knowing look.

'It most certainly is not,' Mandy said indignantly.

'I'm afraid I took the liberty of informing the hotel that you would be checking out today,' he said in a regretful tone that didn't fool her for a second. 'They were very grateful as they have a waiting list. They ask that you clear out your things before midday.'

'Deception last night and bullying this morning,' she seethed. 'So this is how you get your own way.'

'It's the quickest method,' he said, the picture of innocence.

And just for one moment there was a gleam of the old mischief, a hint of teasing challenge in his look. It vanished quickly, as though he'd suppressed it, but she forgave him everything in return for that glimpse of hope.

Since there was nothing else to do, she gave in and returned to the hotel, where she found he'd gone one further and paid her bill. His car ferried her back to his house, a ludicrous waste considering the short distance, but by now she had the picture. He was keeping her where he could see her, just as he'd done the night before.

Now, she told herself, she was nearing the moment when she could tell him about Danny. Perhaps even today.

But she returned to find him deep in a business call. She concentrated on settling into the delightful room Teresa had prepared for her. It had an enormously wide bed that looked at least two hundred years old, and its own bathroom. The windows were traditional, with wooden shutters on the outside that could be drawn to shut out the most determined sunlight.

Ferrini's car collected her again and she spent the rest of the day in his library, returning with a stack of books and papers.

Teresa explained that Renzo would be detained all evening by a business meeting. Mandy was becoming used to his changes of mind, warding her off defensively one moment, drawing her close the next, then warding her off again. It was possible to cope, now that she understood.

She called home night and morning, looking forward to her gurgled conversations with

Danny, picturing his face, so like that of his great-grandfather that she almost told Sue to bring him out here at once.

But not just yet. There lingered in her mind the memory of Renzo saying that his knowledge of family life had scarred him too much to make him a good father. His recent experiences were unlikely to have changed his view. Yet the time was coming when she must take the chance.

One morning, while she was working in Ferrini's house, feeling in dire need of coffee, she went across the hall to the kitchen and just noticed a figure in the shadows, who retreated at once.

'Luigi?' she called. 'Why are you hiding? Don't say you're afraid of me.'

'Not you,' he muttered, emerging. 'Him.'

'Him? Who?'

'Renzo. I don't want to be a dead man.'

'Don't be absurd.'

'You don't know what he said he'd do to me if I troubled you.' Luigi looked around as though fearful that Renzo would be watching them.

'I seem to remember it was me threatening you, not him,' Mandy said.

'No, after that. He called me and said I must stay away from you.'

'He did *what*? Look, he was just being a bit overprotective.'

'I know the difference between a man who's protective and a man who's jealous to the point of murder.' Luigi eyed her cautiously. 'I guess he's not such a dead man.' He retreated back into the shadows. 'Don't tell him we talked. I'm not ready to die.'

She smiled at his comical tone, but she was thoughtful for the rest of the day. That evening she refused the car and walked for a while, not looking where she was going, sunk in thought until she found a bench. There she sat down, took out the photograph of Danny that never left her and gazed at it longingly, missing him so much that she ached.

At last she put it safely away, then took her cellphone and called home to England.

'I don't suppose Danny's awake?' she asked hopefully.

'I've only just got him to sleep,' Sue told her. 'Do you want me to wake him? It would be better not to. He's been a bit upset today. He keeps saying "Mummy" and I tell him he'll see Mummy soon.'

'He will,' Mandy said firmly. 'I've waited long enough. Now it's time for action. Don't wake him now, but call me tomorrow morning.'

It was late when she went home. Teresa was in the hall.

'He's waiting for you,' she said quietly.

As she went into the living room Renzo was standing there.

'Where have you been?' he demanded. 'I've been worried. You might have got lost.'

'No, I wasn't lost. I had things to think about, and decide.'

'And what have you decided?' he asked, sounding tense.

'This,' she said simply, and reached up to kiss him.

She felt the shock go through his body and the next instant his arms were around her, drawing her fiercely against him, telling her with every movement that she was doing the right thing.

'Mandy,' he said hoarsely. 'Tell me—'

'No,' she murmured. 'No more talk. We've talked too much. Kiss me.'

He responded with a vigour that told her he'd wanted this as much as she had. No caution now, no holding back, only a desperate seeking of the dream before it vanished.

But it wasn't going to vanish, she promised him with every caress. It was here for him for ever. Her lips, her hands, her heart told him. As for herself, she'd waited two years for this moment, and nothing was going to take it from her now.

'You're doing something dangerous,' he murmured huskily.

'There's pleasure in going to the edge, remember?' she reminded him. 'We've been to the edge before, but we went over apart and we paid for it. This time we're going over together, and we're going to be rulers of the world, just as you said.'

He looked at her intently. 'Do you mean that?' he asked, half hopeful, half not wanting to hope.

'If we don't, there's nothing else.'

Now she saw something in his eyes that thrilled her. Time had rolled back and he was once more a man alight with an inner fire. His grasp on her hands was tight, drawing her out of the room. At the foot of the stairs he kissed her again, then watched her, waiting for something.

Now it was she who took control. 'Come with me,' she said.

'To the top of the mountain?'

'Where else?'

'And then—'

She gave a laugh of pure triumph. 'Then,' she said, 'we're going to hold hands and jump.'

CHAPTER NINE

THE lights were out in his room, but the shutters stood open, letting in a soft blue glow.

'Don't look at me,' Renzo said.

Mandy was about to protest that his damaged appearance didn't repel her, but she decided that actions would be better than words. And there was another reason, one that attracted her even more.

'Remember the darkness?' she asked him as she drew the shutters closed, blocking out the light. 'There was snow on every side of the hut except the side that was missing. It blocked out all the light, so that we had to use a torch sometimes, and at other times we managed without light.'

'I remember. And the cold.'

'We huddled under blankets and kept warm together.'

'It wasn't cold when you were there. You drove it away.'

She took his hand and laid the fingers on her buttons, letting him know what she wanted. He began to undress her slowly and she felt his fingertips just brushing her skin. The very lightness of that touch drove her wild. She wanted more, and then more. She wanted everything from him, but she forced herself to be patient, though it was hard when she could sense the time coming.

He drew her close, so that her breasts touched his skin, and she felt him tremble. For a while they held each other like that, exchanging warmth and comfort as much as desire. He dropped his head onto her shoulder, which was not easy as she was so much shorter.

'You're so tiny,' he murmured.

'Delicate,' she teased softly.

He gave a choke of laughter. 'Yes, delicate.'

She drew back the duvet and they lay down, hurriedly removing the rest of their clothes and tossing them onto the floor.

'We did this last time,' she reminded him, 'and we had to use the torch to find them the next morning.'

'We couldn't see anything,' he said. 'I held you safe, because I was afraid if I let go, you'd vanish. Don't vanish now.'

'Here I am.'

'I remember this,' he whispered, trailing his fingers over her breasts, down to her tiny waist. 'And you sighed as though you loved it.'

'Mmm, yes, I did. And there was something you loved too—I know that because I was exploring, trying to find what pleased you—this?—or this?—or perhaps a little differently, and I must have got it right because you suddenly yelled—'

'Don't stop!' he said violently. 'Just keep doing that.'

'That's what you said,' she cried joyfully.

She'd begun by meaning to repeat their first love-making as closely as possible, trying to jog his memory, but now there was another avalanche sweeping her away on a torrent of passion and all else was wiped out of her mind.

And then the sweetest thing of all happened. The old connection between their minds was there again, so that she knew what was taking place inside him as clearly as if it were in her own mind. He'd begun with caution, fearful of weakness in his damaged body, but when desire overtook him he forgot everything but the need to love her, claim her.

She gasped with pleasure as he took possession, and she knew him at once. In so many ways he was a stranger, but not now. This was the same man who had loved her two years ago.

His touch was the same, his hot breath on her face, the feel of him between her legs, inside her, seeking, finding, demanding, giving.

As he finally drew away she wanted to cry aloud with triumph and delight. At their deepest, most intimate moments, Renzo had made love to her with the same tenderness and consideration she'd known in him before. Which meant that his true self was still there deep within, and only needed her to call him back to life.

Lying on his back, Renzo kept one hand on her body, unwilling to let go.

But she slipped away from him, out of bed, towards the window, opening the shutters just a little so that a soft light came into the room. It was just enough for him to see her there, a shadowy figure with an air of unreality. He held his breath as she moved towards him, swaying a little until she sat beside him on the bed.

She touched his chest where the scar was just visible, then lay across him so that her cheek was against it. Once he would have flinched from that contact, hating to be seen by someone who remembered him as he once had been. But with her there was no longer fear. There was only peace as the locked doors opened in his mind and he saw who was standing beyond them.

'It was you,' he murmured. 'It was always you.'

'Yes, it was always me.'

'I told you that I loved you,' he said, 'and that I was glad to say it to you and nobody else, that it would always be you, for however long we had.'

'Then you left me,' she said, 'and I thought it was for ever.'

Mandy lifted herself a little and looked down his length, smiling.

'What are you thinking?' he asked.

'What do you think I'm thinking?' she teased.

'I never knew that, and I guess I never will.'

'It wouldn't be so hard to guess this time,' she murmured provocatively.

'Little cat,' he said, seizing her and tossing her onto her back.

'You guessed right.' She chuckled.

Then speech faded and the only sound was a long sigh of satisfaction as she wrapped her arms around his neck, drawing him as close as she could, until they were both drained.

Despite his exhaustion, Renzo felt mysteriously flooded with strength, something he hadn't known for two years and which he'd never expected to know again. At some time in the recent past there might have been pain, tension, misery, but he could no longer remember as he sank into sleep.

Somewhere on the edge of his consciousness there was a little black cat, not running away now, but contentedly licking its paws, with the air of a creature who'd come home.

They were awoken by the sound of the bedside telephone. Renzo answered and Mandy saw a horrified expression come over his face.

'All right, I'll be down fast,' he said, getting out of bed. 'That was Lucia. There are two men waiting in my office, with an appointment. I forgot. Look at the time. I'll see you later.'

He gave her a quick kiss and vanished into his bathroom. Mandy gave a wry smile. She'd pictured their waking differently, perhaps as the moment she could tell him her secret. But she wasn't entirely displeased to have this happen instead. She wondered when Renzo had last slept late and forgotten a business appointment. And the vigour in his movements as he headed for the bathroom suggested that he'd benefited from their night together.

As she gathered her things she noticed a photograph on a shelf by his bed, and wasn't surprised to see Bruno's face, its likeness to Danny even more pronounced.

She was humming as she gathered her things and headed for her own room.

Downstairs, she found Teresa in an impish mood, pouring coffee with an air of triumph. 'I told Lucia not to disturb him,' she said. 'To hell with business. You'll do him more good.'

'Not if he loses a deal,' Mandy remarked. 'I hope you don't get into trouble.'

'That depends on you,' Teresa said mischievously. 'You be nice to him and he won't be cross.'

When she'd finished breakfast there was still no sign of Renzo, so she collected some papers Ferrini had given her and took them out into the garden. The job was proving more rewarding than she'd feared and she read for an hour, although with half her mind she was wondering how Renzo was faring with his neglected clients.

In fact, he was doing well. If Mandy could have been a fly on the wall she would have appreciated the speed and efficiency with which he charmed them out of their annoyance, wrapped up a big order and sent them on their way. Then he went in search of her, quickly spotting her in the garden.

Something about the sight of her sitting in the sun made him smile. He was still smiling as he moved outside and stood beneath a tree, watching her.

Before he could speak, her cellphone rang. She answered, and immediately joy filled her face.

'Hello, darling! Oh, how lovely to hear from you! I was about to call you, just to hear your voice. What's that? Yes, I miss you too. I'm just longing for us to be together again—for always and always. I love you—if only you knew how much I love you. Do you love me? Truly? Say it again—just one more time.'

Renzo, hearing every word, watching her radiant with happiness, felt a slow death creeping inside him. He should move away. It was shocking to eavesdrop. Yet stone weights held him to the spot.

She laughed, and the sound went through him, ripping him apart as it went. Much worse was the way she threw back her head as though yielding to some blissful satisfaction.

In just such a way had she lain beneath him last night, her head tossed back in eager abandon, offering him her very vulnerability as a gift. How he had loved her for that! How easy it had been then to offer his own vulnerability in return, something he'd never done before in his life.

He'd trusted her. And all the time—

The thought that she'd seen him defenceless brought him so close to violent rage that he began to retreat into the shadows, desperate to get away lest he do her harm.

Mandy neither saw nor heard him. All her attention was for the phone and the gurgling voice of her son until the gurgles turned into a shriek of laughter, and Sue took his place.

'He was talking to me,' Mandy said. 'Real words.'

'Of course he was.' Sue laughed. 'I definitely heard "Duh" and "Ugh".'

'Oh, ye of little faith. He said he loved me, and then he said it again. Wait until you're a mother, then you'll know.'

'I believe you. How are things going there? Have you told him yet?'

'No, but I'm nearly there.'

They talked about domestic things for a while, then she hung up and sat contentedly, musing on her happiness. She was close—very close—to her heart's desire.

Then, as she glanced around the courtyard, something strange happened. Although she was alone she had a sudden irrational conviction that somebody had been standing there beneath the tree. There was nobody there now, yet the conviction persisted.

She went inside to the kitchen, where Teresa was making more coffee.

'Is Renzo still in the office?' Mandy asked.

'No, that's him in the hall, heading upstairs,' Teresa replied. 'He seems to be in a rush.'

Running upstairs, Mandy saw Renzo's bedroom door open. He was inside, sitting on the bed, and when he looked up she was shocked. His face was grey, tight and harsh.

'Renzo, what is it? What's happened?'

His eyes were like stones. 'Perhaps I should be asking you that question.'

She moved nearer. 'I don't understand.'

He rose and moved away as though he didn't want to be too close to her.

'I thought I'd found the one trustworthy woman in all the world,' he said softly. 'More fool me. I should have asked you questions, shouldn't I?'

'What kind of questions?' she asked, stunned by the hatred in his eyes.

'About you. About your life. About who you're sleeping with these days. You know all about me, but I've taken you on trust.'

'And now you think you shouldn't have done?' she asked, angry in her turn. 'Are you going to tell me why?'

'With pleasure. And when I've done that I'm going to throw you out with even more pleasure, and after that I never want to hear of or see you again. Because I don't forgive. I thought you were…different. You made me think so back then, and again when you turned up here. But you just wanted to make a fool of me.'

She was too appalled to speak. This was the man she'd seen that first day—bitter, savagely angry, looking at her with something like hate.

Mandy's head was whirling but she forced herself to be calm. She couldn't afford to weaken now. She'd never seen so much concentrated fury in anyone's face—and the sight of it directed at herself, from the man who'd loved her so tenderly the night before, filled her with dread.

'Renzo, wait,' she said. 'Listen to me.'

'Listen to you? I never want to hear another word you say.'

'But how has this happened—after last night?'

'Don't dare mention that. Last night I believed in you, believed you might actually love me.'

'But I—'

'Don't say it. I couldn't bear to listen. Did you enjoy last night? Did it give you a good laugh? Did you call *him* afterwards and joke about how easily you tricked me? Or did you just snigger inside at how easily I succumbed?'

'You must be quite mad to talk like that,' she said, growing angry. 'Why would I trick you? Why would I want to?'

'I can't imagine. Why don't you tell me? *Why did you come here?*'

'Because I spent two years grieving for you. I cried myself to sleep night after night because

I thought you were dead. Those last two days we had together you were different, marvellous. I fell in love with you and it nearly drove me out of my mind when I thought you were gone.

'When I heard you were alive I couldn't just leave things there. I had to find you and know if you remembered me, if you were the same man—'

'Don't tell me lies,' he said contemptuously. 'It was an end game, wasn't it? You did what you liked with me last time, and you had to prove you could do it again. Well, you did. Congratulations on your success. I jumped through all the hoops, didn't I?'

'*Renzo*—'

'To think I carried you in my heart as a beautiful dream, someone too lovely to exist. Shall I tell you what happened to me after I fell? I lay in that frozen place for a time I can't even guess. I was in such pain that I prayed for death. I thought you were dead too and after the time we spent together I didn't want to live without you.

'I saw you. You were there, beckoning me on, taking me to the place where you were, and we could be together for ever. I felt myself reaching out to you. I couldn't have done because my whole body was trapped, frozen, but my heart reached out. I'd have followed you anywhere.'

'Why did you never tell me this before?' she cried in anguish.

'Because it was wiped from my brain by everything that happened afterwards. I forgot it as though it had never happened. When I awoke I had only fractured memories that I couldn't understand.

'But last night everything came back to me as clearly as if it were yesterday. I lay in your arms after we made love and I was back there, buried under the snow again—everthing was the same except that there was no pain. You were with me, beckoning just as before, but not to death—to life. A whole new world opened because you were with me.'

He closed his eyes suddenly, as though the memories were more than he could bear.

'Renzo,' she whispered, going to him.

'Stay away from me,' he snapped, opening his eyes again. 'Don't touch me, don't come near me. Just listen. I'd forgotten everything except my confused fantasies, but when you first came here and I finally saw you, it seemed that the fantasies were reality. I didn't want to believe it. I tried to be cautious, to warn myself that no woman could be trusted, but I couldn't help myself. Against my own will, I trusted you. That will teach me to be more careful in future.'

'For pity's sake, where does all this come from? Where did you get these crazy ideas?'

'Do you know how much I'd give to believe they really were crazy? If only I could turn the clock back to before I heard you, and make it not happen!'

'Heard me? Heard what?'

'In the garden a few minutes ago. You should be more careful about taking phone calls.'

'You were down there,' she breathed. 'I thought so, but then I couldn't see you.'

'Or you'd have been more careful,' he raged.

'About what?'

'Calling him "darling", telling him you loved him.' He suddenly moved close to her, his eyes deadly. 'Last night it was me you loved, or so you said. Today it's him. Who's in line for tomorrow?'

Mandy clenched her hands, close to hitting him for the desecration of what had been perfect. For a moment every feeling was expunged except a hatred that was as fierce as his own.

'I'm going to make you sorry you said that,' she breathed.

'That's doubtful. I enjoyed it too much.'

'I'll bet you did. Well, here's something else for you to enjoy. You want to know who I was talking to? His name is Danny Jenkins.'

He paled. 'Your husband?'

'My son.'

That checked him, but only for a moment. 'Really?' he queried with an emphasis of contempt. 'Are you going to tell me who his father is?'

'I'll do better. I'll *show* you who his great-grandfather is.'

She snatched up the picture of Renzo's grandfather from the bedside table, thrust it into his hands, then opened her purse, took out the snapshot of Danny that she always kept with her and held that before him.

'This is my son,' she raged. 'Danny—short for Danilo.'

Slowly Renzo sat down, clicking from one picture to the other, with their likeness so pronounced that Mandy knew that he couldn't doubt the child was his. But now she hated herself.

She'd dreamed of how she would tell him—gently, lovingly. She'd pictured his happiness as he understood the new hope that had opened before him.

And in the end she'd hurled everything at him in bitter, cruel rage and now nothing would ever be right again. She wanted to howl and bang her head against the wall.

She looked at Renzo, wondering what damage she might have done with her clumsiness. He'd placed the snapshot on top of his grandfather's picture so that he could see them together. He seemed transfixed.

'He was born at the end of October,' she said. 'Just nine months after we were together. Renzo—'

She touched his shoulder, worried by his silence.

'I have…a son,' he whispered.

She dropped to her knees beside him. '*We* have a son,' she said. 'Yours and mine. I used to wish he looked like you, but he's the image of your grandfather.'

'It never occurred to me…' he murmured. 'I just thought of myself, didn't I? All this time… Why didn't you tell me before?'

'Because I couldn't. The day I arrived and saw how you were, how could I have told you then? You'd have thrown me out—' she gave a faint wry smile '—even faster than you actually did.

'Ever since then I've been waiting for the right moment, but it didn't come. You couldn't remember that we'd made love, and without that you might not have believed me.

'But after last night I hoped. I was going to tell you this morning, but you had to hurry away. Then Sue called me—she's the friend who's taking care of Danny—and she put him straight on. We talk every day. He can manage quite a few words, and the rest of the time he gurgles. I talk to him as though he can understand everything. He's so bright.'

'You called him Danilo,' he murmured.

'What else should I call him? He's yours. In here—' she touched her heart '—you never died. I couldn't let you go, and you're there in Danny. He's a beautiful baby. Just wait until you see him.'

'When will that be?'

'I'll call Sue and she can bring him over. It's probably too late for her to travel today, but tomorrow. Before I left England I fixed him up with a passport so that he could travel at a moment's notice. I was always going to bring him—if you wanted him.'

'If?' he breathed. 'Please, get him here as soon as you can. We've lost too much time already.'

She called Sue, who promised to call back when she'd booked tickets. An hour later it was all sorted.

'Tomorrow,' Mandy said, hanging up. 'The flight lands at midday.'

Renzo didn't reply in words and she wondered if he'd heard, but the next moment he embraced her in a hug so fierce that it almost squeezed the breath out of her.

'We'll be there,' he said fiercely and walked away, leaving her standing alone.

Mandy was too wise to follow him. It would have been wonderful to laugh and rejoice together, but she knew by now that this was a deeply troubled man and there was still some distance to travel. For the moment it was enough that he was glad about his son.

She found Teresa, told her everything and smiled at the older woman's beaming delight.

'I get a room ready for your friend,' she said. 'There's a nice one right next to yours.'

It was a perfect choice. The room was large and airy. Teresa had a maid cleaning it out within minutes, decorating it with flowers until it was fit for a queen. Mandy gave her an impulsive kiss of gratitude and only wished she could call Renzo to see how his household was preparing for his son.

She didn't meet him for the rest of the day. As dusk fell she looked out of the window and saw him in the garden by the fountain, staring into the water.

By late evening she still hadn't spoken to him, and sadly she decided to go to bed. She heard him go to his own room and the door close with a depressing sound of finality.

But a moment later there came a soft knock

on her door, and when she opened it she found him looking like a man who wasn't sure of his welcome.

'I'm sorry to disturb you,' he said.

'You can disturb me any time you like, surely you know that?' When he didn't move she took his hand. 'Come in.'

He let her draw him in until they were both sitting on the bed, but when she tried to kiss him he stopped her.

'Don't you have something you want to say to me first?'

'About what?'

'About the way I behaved this morning, hurling abuse at you after last night.'

'Perhaps remembering last night made it worse. We were so close, and if you thought I'd betrayed you—'

'You're very generous, but we both know I was out of control. I was cruel. I've never thought of myself as a cruel man, but I said terrible things just to hurt you. Can you forgive me?'

'There's nothing to forgive.'

'Yes, there is. I shouldn't have flown at you like that. I should have asked you calmly who you'd been talking to.'

She could almost have laughed at the way he said 'calmly'.

'You could have been calm if you didn't care,' she said gently. 'Let it go. There's no harm done.'

She spoke confidently but in her heart she knew that it wasn't really that simple. Somewhere in a distant place in his mind Renzo's demons were still howling. And he knew it. And was afraid.

CHAPTER TEN

'THERE'S no harm done,' Mandy repeated gently. 'You're not a cruel man, just one who's been very ill, and isn't well yet.'

'That's nice of you, but—'

'Renzo, stop it. You can't blame yourself for everything, especially with me. Who knows better than I do what you've been through? And even I only half know. I didn't suffer anywhere near as much as you did, but we know things that other people have never dreamed of, and we don't have to explain ourselves to each other.'

He was about to speak again but she silenced him, drawing him towards the bed and down onto it. Now he was content to follow her lead, letting her undress him and reaching to undress her, but she was ahead of him, eager to be naked with him, eager to love him, because only her love could ease his darkened mind.

She went slowly, waiting for him to relax,

teasing and enticing until he was ready to take command, then yielding herself up to him with joy. At last she had what she wanted when she looked into his face and knew that she had driven care from his mind.

But perhaps not for long. She knew the demons would return. She prayed that she would be powerful enough to banish them for good, but when she tried to look into the future she saw a twisted road with no sign where it led.

Afterwards, he lay in her arms. 'How could I ever have forgotten making love to you?' Renzo asked in a wondering tone. 'It's all clear now, everything—it was so cold that we had to huddle together for warmth, and so dark that we couldn't see each other. It's all come back.'

'That's what really matters,' Mandy told him fondly.

'We thought we were going to die,' he mused, 'and all I wanted was you.'

'For however long we have—and after-wards,' she reminded him.

'Yes, I said that. And you said you loved me. Do you remember?'

'I remember,' she whispered, kissing him.

'What happened when you got back to England, when you found you were pregnant?'

'Sue was living with me by then. She's a

nurse and she was doing agency work, just accepting temporary jobs so that she could look after me at the same time.

'She spotted that I was pregnant. I thought I was just having dizzy spells after what had happened, but she made me see the truth. On the very same day I read in the paper that you were dead and buried.

'Until then, I'd clung to the hope that you might still be alive. After that, it was only Danny who helped me to go on living. It meant you'd left me part of yourself, and he was doubly precious.

'I used to talk to him about his father, even before he was born, and more afterwards. If you really had been dead, he'd still have grown up knowing about you. But now—' she gave a happy sigh '—now you'll get to know each other as father and son. It's going to be marvellous.'

'Is it?'

An odd note in his voice made her look at him quickly.

'You have more faith in me than I have in myself,' he said quietly. 'How can I ever be a father?'

'You *are* a father,' Mandy insisted.

'Only in name. You've managed very well without me so far.'

'Oh, no, we haven't,' she said fervently. 'We haven't managed well without you at all. There's always been a great gap where you belonged. You're Danny's father. Nothing can take that away.'

When he didn't answer, she shook his shoulders gently.

'Renzo, what's the matter? When I told you, you couldn't wait to see him.'

'Yes, that was my first impulse, but since then I've been thinking. I told you once that with all I've got in here—' he tapped his breast '—I'd better not have children.'

'Until you were too old and decrepit to do anything else,' she said lightly. 'Well, I'm glad we dispensed with that one.'

He smiled, but he was still troubled.

'I'm just not sure I can cope with a family,' he said. 'I told you a little about my experience of family life and I dare say Teresa has filled you in about the rest.'

'She added a few things,' Mandy agreed.

'So you'll know that it's something that makes me nervous. Parents and children   how they relate to each other—I just don't know.'

'What about your father? Even when your mother left, you still had him.'

'His way of coping was to let me do as I liked

while he got on with his own life. I didn't have any complaints at the time. No child is going to object to having his own way, but we ended up barely acquainted. When it comes to being a father—I know nothing.'

'And neither does any other man with his first child,' Mandy tried to reassure him. 'You learn as you go along. And you did have some family life, with your grandfather. Teresa told me he adored you, that he gave you the only love you really had in your childhood. You adored him too, didn't you? That's why his is the only picture you keep.'

He nodded reflectively. 'If I hadn't had him to cling to, things would have been even worse. He gave me security, and when I grew up he invested in me with a loan to start the business, no interest and unsecured. Later, when I tried to pay him back, he didn't want it. He said I should keep it as a gift. I couldn't let him do that, but he wouldn't take the money.'

He grinned suddenly. 'We had a historic battle. I paid the money direct into his bank and he hit the roof. We yelled at each other for a while, he wrote a cheque and stuffed it into my hand. I tore it up. He stormed off and deposited money directly into my bank. Then we had another yelling match.'

'Who gave in?' she asked, much entertained.

'Me, of course. Nobody ever got the better of the old man. The best I managed was to make him accept a partnership in the business so that he had something to show for his money, and I paid him regular dividends. To this day he owns a quarter, and at least I can say he's prospered. But if he'd gone bankrupt he wouldn't have held it against me.

'One day soon I'd like to take you both to see him. He's very old. He spends most of his life asleep, but we might be lucky and catch him on a good day.'

'Yes, I'd love to meet him. And he definitely ought to be introduced to his great-grandson.'

'I wish he was still well enough to be there for Danny. He'd be a better father than I will. I don't think I have the patience— Mandy, you know what I'm trying to say. I can be very difficult. You've discovered that.'

'Yes, with people you think are trying to deceive you. I don't think you need worry about that with Danny.'

'You're so sure, aren't you? Far more than I am.'

'Maybe I know you better than you know yourself.'

'And if I can't find a place in my heart for him? Face it, Mandy, it might happen.'

'Then…' She hesitated, unwilling to confront the thought, but knowing it had to be done. 'If that happened,' she said slowly, 'then Danny and I would have to go away and trouble you no more.'

Renzo drew a sharp breath and his hand tightened slightly on hers, as though he were trying to prevent her escape.

'I couldn't stay here then,' she said sadly. 'Because eventually Danny would know that you didn't love him, and he'd suffer the same kind of rejection that you did. I couldn't do that to him. I'd have to take him away, wouldn't I?'

He nodded, and there was infinite sadness in his face.

'Yes,' he said sadly. 'That's what you'd have to do.'

They were both at the airport the next day. Earlier in the day Renzo had declined to go there, using business as an excuse. Mandy guessed the real reason. He didn't want to meet his son for the first time in public.

But when she looked into his office to say goodbye he suddenly announced that business could wait and came out to the car with her.

'It would look rude if we didn't both welcome your friend,' he said.

She wasn't fooled by that, either. He might pretend as much as he liked. He couldn't wait to see Danny.

It was a good omen, she told herself. As they rode in the back of the car to the airport she was full of hope.

The plane was on time and they had only to position themselves by the gate and wait for Sue to appear.

'Just a few more minutes,' she said excitedly. 'Renzo—where are you?'

He'd moved a few feet behind her. 'I'll wait here,' he said, 'while you say hello.'

It sounded reasonable enough, but it meant that once again he'd withdrawn to watch from a distance. Mandy tried not to be uneasy. He was bound to be cautious.

Then she saw Sue coming towards them, carrying Danny, and all else was forgotten in the joy of seeing them. As she ran forward, Danny spotted her and began wriggling free, yelling, 'Muuu—meee—*Миииии*—'

'Darling,' she cried, taking him from Sue. 'You didn't forget me. Give me a kiss—there—there—my gorgeous boy.'

'Thank goodness you took him before he escaped,' Sue said, laughing and flexing her arm. 'He's getting heavy.'

'Allow me to help with your luggage, *signorina*,' said a quiet voice. 'I am Renzo Ruffini.'

'Where are my manners?' Mandy said guiltily. 'I took one look at Danny and everything went out of my head.'

'Very natural,' Renzo said.

'This is Sue. I've told you about her, and she's been looking after Danny while I was away. And this—is Danny.'

Father and son stared at each other in silence.

Then Renzo said, 'We're holding people up. Let's get out to the car.'

In the car home Mandy sat with Danny on her lap, hugging him and resting her cheek against his head, happy in their reunion but longing to reach home. Renzo was talking to Sue, asking polite questions, seemingly interested in the answers, but Mandy could sense that he was filled with tension.

At last the car drew up. As they entered the house Teresa appeared, beaming a welcome and offering to show Sue up to her room. Sue went with her willingly, knowing that the others needed to be alone.

Renzo followed her into the front room and closed the door.

'Here he is,' Mandy said, turning so that he

could see his son clearly. 'Doesn't he look like your grandfather?'

'Yes, his face is very like,' Renzo agreed.

'He's one year and three months old, and he's got a real personality. He likes his own way and if he doesn't get it he lets you know how he feels.'

'I believe I was much the same.'

'From what I hear, you still are,' she said with an attempt at humour.

'Like father, like son,' he said in the same spirit.

It was all wrong, she thought with a sinking heart. He was doing his best, but it was a palpable effort.

'Would you like to hold him?' she asked.

'I'd be afraid to drop him.'

'Sit on the sofa and I'll give him to you.'

He sat down and she sat beside him, easing Danny into his arms.

But the child promptly let out a bellow and began to struggle, so that she retrieved him hastily.

'He's tired,' she said. 'He needs a nap before he meets people.'

'Of course,' Renzo said, with something in his voice that might have been relief. 'I'll leave you two together, while I get on with some work.'

He departed quickly.

It was too soon, Mandy told herself. Renzo was bound to be wary at first. He just needed time. But she was haunted by the sight of him at the airport, seeing her embrace her son, pouring out motherly love, something that had never happened to him. With all her heart she longed to welcome him into the magic circle, but only he could decide when the moment had come. Until then, he was condemned to stand apart.

Then Danny clamoured for her attention and for a few hours she was able to forget everything but the joy of their reunion. Everyone in the house wanted to meet him, so she had to take him everywhere. The maids lined up to make joyful noises, which Danny returned with interest.

Teresa had outdone herself, reviving every baby-food recipe that she'd ever known, and laying out the details for inspection. Mandy ventured to suggest that for tonight Danny had better stick to his regular diet, which Sue had thoughtfully brought with her. But this was met with outrage.

In order to keep the peace, she made a choice, silently resolving to keep his normal food ready in reserve. But Danny was fast learning the social rules, and from his perch on Mandy's lap he ate everything Teresa offered him with evident enjoyment.

'He's so sweet and well-behaved,' she purred.

'Don't count on that lasting.' Mandy chuckled.

'I think the journey tired him, because usually he's a little devil.'

'Good,' Teresa said fervently. 'That's how it should be. Just like his father.'

She beamed approval at Renzo, who smiled back dutifully.

'It's time he was in bed,' Mandy said, rising with Danny in her arms.

'Shall I come and help you?' Sue asked.

'Thank you, but no. We have a lot of catching up to do. Come along, my little man.'

She dropped a kiss on Danny's head as she carried him out of the room. Renzo watched until they were out of sight, then turned back to Sue and became the perfect host. But Sue had a kind heart and soon released him, declaring herself tired after the journey.

Teresa had celebrated Danny's arrival by ordering the most expensive cot and bedclothes she could find, putting them on Renzo's account and demanding that they be delivered that day on pain of dire retribution. The intimidated store staff had obliged and the cot was waiting in Mandy's room.

'Look at that,' she told him. 'See how welcome they're making you. Oh, let me hug you. It's been so long. Mmm!'

Danny made a sound halfway between a

giggle and a gurgle and she kissed him again and again, murmuring, 'I've really got you back, my darling, and everything's all right again. I'm never going to let you go.'

'Fish,' Danny said firmly.

'Yes, fish. And fish. And fish. All the fish you want. Hey, don't pull my hair.'

She burst out laughing at Danny's determined assault, and he laughed with her.

'I love you, love you, love you!' she said fervently. 'Now, let's get you tucked up and off to sleep. And don't worry, I'm staying right here with you all night.'

She settled Danny in the cot, gazing down with adoration, so oblivious to everything else that she never saw the man standing in the doorway, waiting for her to notice him and smile in welcome. When she didn't, he moved quietly away.

They both wanted Sue to remain for a while and she settled in as part of the family. Renzo visited Danny twice a day, smiled and said the right things, but always with a kind of reserve that Mandy sensed he was trying to overcome, but without success.

Again, she found herself remembering the words he'd spoken in the mountains.

'A man who takes such a jaundiced view of families as I do had probably better not have children.'

Had he spoken more prophetically than he knew? He'd been pleased with the idea of Danny but, as he'd warned her, the reality made him uneasy.

As a gesture of gratitude, she took Sue shopping in the Via Montenapoleone. They were alone, having yielded to Teresa's pleas for Danny to be left with her. She bought her friend some costly outfits and they returned home happily to reclaim Danny from the housemaids who were cheerfully neglecting their work to play with him.

But there was no sign of Renzo.

'He's gone to visit the old man,' Teresa confided. 'He always stays with him a long time.'

And it was very late when she heard Renzo return to his room. She knocked on his door and he opened it at once.

'I was wondering if it was too late to disturb you. Come in.'

When he'd closed the door he said, 'I've been to see Nonno,' using the Italian word for Grandfather, and indicating the picture that she'd used to prove Danny's heritage.

'How did you find him?'

'Drifting in and out of consciousness. I tried to tell him about Danny but I'm not sure I got through to him.'

'Then perhaps it's time we all went together,' Mandy suggested.

'I was hoping you'd say that. We'll go tomorrow.'

The care home where Bruno was living was a pleasant country house on the edge of Milan. He was on the ground floor, in a room with large windows with a view of the grounds. He wasn't, as Mandy had expected, in bed, but sitting on a sofa, looking out at the lawn.

She could see that he was very old, with a wizened look, but when he heard them enter he opened his eyes and smiled. His mouth just shaped the word, 'Renzo.'

'You didn't expect to see me back so soon, did you?' Renzo said cheerfully. 'But I told you about my son, and now I want you to meet him.'

For a moment they weren't sure that he'd understood, but then he turned his head slowly to look at Mandy, who'd seated herself beside him on the sofa, with Danny in her arms. Renzo drew up a chair facing them.

'Danilo,' he said, touching the child.

'Danilo.' It was a whisper, barely audible.

'Mandy.' Renzo indicated her.

Bruno might be dreadfully weak, but he was still a gentleman. He inclined his head courteously, and she did the same.

'Renzo has told me…a little about you… not much.' His smile became conspiratorial. 'Now…you tell.'

She gave a brief description of their meeting in the mountains, and their last nights.

'I thought he was dead,' she finished. 'When I discovered that he was alive I came to find him, and tell him about our child.'

'And this…is Renzo's…son?'

'Yes.'

Bruno put out a hand tentatively, and Danny promptly seized it hard enough to make him wince. Renzo instinctively reached out to break the contact.

'No,' Bruno said in a much firmer voice than before. 'It's good. He is strong…break things…'

'Yes,' Mandy said, smiling. 'He does break things.'

'Then he has spirit. In time…he will build things. I remember…' the old man's eyes rested warmly on Renzo '…when he wanted to smash everything, but he recovered.'

'Because of you,' Mandy said.

'No, because of himself.' Bruno looked at

Renzo. 'He will be to you what you have been to me.'

'Will he?' Renzo murmured, and Mandy wondered if she really heard a wistful note in his voice.

'We never think so at first,' Bruno said gently. 'We see only the difficulty, the little terror who breaks our tools and makes a mess. But then there is the smile—you'll see it soon, and know that it is just for you. After that—there is nothing you will not do to keep him safe.'

He stroked Danny's forehead. 'Thank you for bringing him to me.'

'I'll go out for a while,' Mandy said.

When they were alone, Bruno said, 'So she is the one.'

'Yes,' Renzo said quietly. 'She is the one.'

'She will be good for you. When will you marry?'

'I don't know. I haven't asked her yet.'

'Don't let her slip through your fingers. When you've found the one, you must secure her. Not just because of the child. If you lose her, you'll regret it all your life.'

'I know that, Nonno, but I've changed. I see myself clearly and I don't like myself. That gap in there—' he pointed to his chest '—I'm afraid I'm not fit to be a husband or a father.'

'They will make you fit,' Bruno said.

'I'll let them down, and I could never forgive myself for that,' Renzo said desperately.

'You're afraid you'll do to them what was done to you,' Bruno said wisely, and Renzo nodded. 'But never fear. They won't let you. They'll draw you out into the world of trust and love. Even if you don't trust yourself, trust the woman you love, and the child she bore you. They'll never fail you.'

'I know. Don't worry, Nonno. I know the only happiness lies with them.'

'Then I have nothing left to hope for,' Bruno murmured. His eyes began to close. 'I'm tired. Let me sleep now.'

His eyes closed slowly. Renzo kissed his cheek and went out of the room, nodding to the nurse to go in.

'Thank you,' he said quietly to Mandy.

In the back of the car going home he said little, but he looked at Danny constantly, and there was a faint smile on his face. Mandy watched them both, silent and content.

CHAPTER ELEVEN

WHEN they reached home Renzo vanished into his office, saying that he must catch up on work. Mandy would have liked to talk to him about what had happened, but clearly he didn't want that. She spent the evening chatting with Sue before looking in to say goodnight to him. He smiled briefly and returned to work.

'This afternoon I thought things were getting better,' she confided to Sue as they climbed the stairs. 'But we take one step forward and two steps back.'

'And if it doesn't come right?' Sue ventured. 'What happens then?'

'I don't know,' she said with a sigh.

But she did know. And the thought of the decision that she might be facing filled her with sadness.

It was the height of summer. The heat could become intolerable during the day, and scarcely less so at night, so that both the windows and the shutters were left open. On a moonlit night the bedroom never became entirely dark.

Having seen Danny settled in his cot, Mandy stretched out on the bed, wearing a nightdress that was barely a whisper and with only a sheet to cover her. Even so, she was still too hot and slept fitfully.

She awoke suddenly, wondering what was different. The room was silent, yet she knew something strange had happened, piercing her sleep. Then she turned her head and saw Renzo.

He was sitting by the cot, gazing down into it, totally still. She waited for him to glance her way, but he didn't. His attention was all for the child and she might not have existed. When he finally moved, it was only to lean down further, peering intently. Mandy could just make out his face with its faint smile that widened suddenly, as though something new and delightful had caught his attention. When his head turned a little she could see that his eyes were gleaming, not only with pleasure, but with something that was almost triumph.

A man marvelling at newly discovered treasure might gaze at it with that reverent wonder—half joy, half disbelief. Mandy lay still, her heart beating so loudly that she feared he might hear it, but he was totally absorbed in his son.

Now she understood what he had meant about seeing without being seen. It was a pleasure to study him without his knowledge. He was bare-chested, and in this light the scars were invisible, leaving only the lithe, strongly built man she remembered from a time that sometimes seemed like another world.

A sound from the cot showed that Danny had awoken. At once Renzo pressed a finger to his lips and pointed to the bed. Danny began to make grumbling noises, which caused Renzo to shush him frantically.

'*Silenzio!*' he whispered. 'Don't wake Mamma.'

But the sounds increased.

'I think you'd better wake Mamma,' Mandy told him.

Renzo jumped, then gave her a quick look that was almost guilty. 'I thought you were asleep.'

'I was. You must have entered very quietly not to have disturbed me. How long have you been there?'

'I'm not sure, perhaps an hour. I came in because I hoped you were awake. I didn't knock in case I awoke him too, but you were both asleep. I suppose I should have gone away—'

'You know better than that,' she said at once. 'You don't need permission to visit your own son.'

'I meant to waken you, but I got to looking at him lying there, and then I couldn't stop.'

She sat up in the bed. 'It was lovely. You were doing so well.'

'Was I? I've never talked to a baby before. I don't understand their language.'

'You pick it up as you go along,' she said, pushing back the sheet. 'Then, gradually you get to understand each other. When he says this—' she gave a grunt '—it means he wants to be changed. I'll show you how to do it.'

'Show…me?' he said, with the gulping horror of fathers since the dawn of time.

'Well, you're obviously training to be the perfect father. What better moment for a lesson?'

But, at the sight of his appalled face, she relented. 'It's all right. I'll let you off this time.'

She went into her little bathroom and did what was necessary. He came to the door to watch, but only from a safe distance.

'Coward,' she jeered, chuckling.

'Definitely.'

When she'd finished, she laid Danny in his father's arms.

'Hold him for me while I get washed,' she said, returning to the bathroom.

She took her time washing, turned out the bathroom light and slipped back into the bedroom unnoticed. She had her reward in the sight of Danny sitting on Renzo's lap, supported by his arm, looking up with an appraising expression.

'He's not sure what he makes of you,' she said, laughing softly.

'What about what I make of him?' Renzo demanded.

'That doesn't bother him nearly as much. He knows the opinion that matters is his. He'll inform you when he's ready.'

He grinned. 'Got it all sussed, huh?'

'You'd better believe it. He's going to go through life afraid of nobody.'

Renzo studied his son's face, and nodded. 'Yes, I think that's what he's trying to tell me. What are you doing now?'

Mandy had gone to a bedside cupboard and taken out a small bottle and a cup.

'He likes a little drink of orange juice when he wakes at night,' she explained, pouring juice into the cup and setting it down. 'I keep this in the fridge by day, and take it out when I come to bed. By the time he's ready for it, the chill has gone.'

She sat down on the bed and reached out to take Danny from him. The child went willingly, but kept his eyes on Renzo, evidently regarding him as a curiosity. They had been acquainted for several days now, yet Mandy had the strange sense that each was seeing the other for the first time.

'Now, perhaps Poppa will hand us the cup,' she said.

Renzo entered into the spirit, pointing to himself and repeating, 'Poppa.'

Danny frowned.

'Poppa,' Renzo said again.

At last Danny made his decision. 'Fish,' he announced.

'Hey, that's my word,' Mandy protested. 'I'm your fish. You said so.'

'Fish,' Danny repeated firmly.

'But I'm an Italian fish,' Renzo declared. *'Pesce.'*

'Fish.'

'Pesce.'

'Argue it out some other time,' Mandy said hastily. 'Now, if Signor Pesce will give you the cup.'

Signor Pesce duly obliged, holding it out to Danny, who reached out for it, floundering but determined.

'I'd better take it,' Mandy said, laughing.

With a little help, Danny managed to get both hands on the cup and aim it roughly at his mouth to take a long satisfying drink. Then he gazed defiantly at his mother, as if to say, *See!*

'Oh, yes, you're very clever,' she told him. 'You don't have to tell me. I know you are. And now you're going to prove it by going back to sleep.'

His defiance didn't waver, but his eyes began to close.

'I guess you won that one,' Renzo said softly.

'It's not hard. He's worked out that the more he sleeps, the better mayhem he can create tomorrow. Come on, my darling.'

She laid Danny back in his cot. He was already asleep.

'He looks so innocent,' Renzo said in wonder.

'It's a trick. That's how he fools you. You don't find out he's actually a villain until it's too late and he's got a grip on your heart. Ask Bruno.'

He laughed softly. 'I know. Nonno always said I practised a *Who, me?* look. He said the more innocent I seemed the more alarmed he became.'

'I know exactly what he means,' she said tenderly.

After a moment he said, 'Thank you for today. Nonno doesn't have much left to hope for in his life, and you gave him something that made him happy.'

'No, it was you who did that.'

'Don't flatter me. You've had the hard part, I know—bearing Danny and raising him alone. How did you ever do it?'

'I did it for you,' she said simply. 'You were always there with me. I was never alone.'

'Never alone,' he said slowly. 'How could I be with you, and not know?'

'Perhaps you did know, in your heart,' she said slowly.

He nodded thoughtfully but said no more. Danny stirred, and he glanced back at him.

'You said he was born in October.'

She gave him the exact date.

'Was it very hard?'

'It took a long time. First babies often do. Once they thought something was going wrong and I was terrified in case I lost him. But Sue was there, holding my hand, and it was all right in the end. I couldn't have borne to lose him. It would have been like losing you all over again.'

'I should have been there,' he whispered. '*Mio dio*, it should have been me holding your hand.'

'Yes,' she said sadly. 'You should have been

the first one to see him and hold him. You should have been there when he cut his first tooth at seven months. Wait, I'll show you.'

She put on the bedside light and got up, reaching into a drawer and pulled out a book which she opened for him, showing it to be a photo album.

'Sue brought it with her,' she said.

Renzo was staring at the picture on the first page.

'But—that's me,' he said, thunderstruck. 'How could you possibly have my photograph?'

'Low cunning,' she said. 'Never fails. When we were in the mountains I could take pictures with my cellphone. I took several of you, without you knowing. When the rescue party found me in the hut they found my things, as well, and the cellphone was there. After I returned to England, I had the pictures developed. That was the best, but there were some other nice ones.'

Renzo turned the page and saw himself as he'd been then, in climbing gear, laughing, game for action, king of the world.

'I wonder who he was,' he mused. 'I don't know him. He looks a paltry fellow, the sort who'd swing off balconies and think he was being clever.'

'Oh, he had his good moments,' she said in a considering voice. 'I can't remember them right now, but he must have had something.'

'Thank you, ma'am,' he said, grinning.

But then his grin faded as he turned the page and saw a picture of Mandy, taken in the hospital, holding the day-old Danny. Watching his face she saw an expression of unutterable sadness that only deepened as he went through the book and saw more pictures.

There was Danny at his christening, sleeping soundly in his mother's arms, then sitting up in his high chair, clearly older and bigger, beaming mischievously. And, just behind him, was the enlarged picture of his father.

More pictures, all telling the same story, of a child growing quickly in strength, health and intelligence. And every time Renzo's photograph could be seen, never far from his son, as if watching over him.

'You kept me alive for him,' he whispered.

'I tried to. It helped me too. I had someone to talk to.'

He wondered if she knew how the unconscious inflection in her voice had betrayed the depths of her loneliness. But she wouldn't know, he guessed. There had never been anyone less given to self-pity than her.

'Why didn't you show me this earlier?' he asked.

'I've always wanted to. It wasn't the right moment before. But tonight…it was.'

Tonight he'd begun to open his heart to his child and she was alive with hope.

He was turning the pages, lingering over a picture of Danny with a warm smile.

'They say babies start being shy of strangers after a few months,' Mandy said, 'but he never was. His attitude was always *bring 'em on*.'

'So much I missed,' he mused. 'Lost for ever.'

'But there's much more still to come,' she reminded him. 'A lifetime. You don't have to miss that.'

'A lifetime.' He looked at her across the cot. 'Do you really think you could put up with me for a lifetime?'

'Try me.'

'You were always brave, but you'd need all the courage in the world to take me on.'

'It would take far more courage to live without you,' she told him softly. 'That's what I can't face.'

He came to sit beside her on the bed and spoke fervently. 'Do you remember when I said I loved you back then?'

'Every word.'

'I never thought I'd get the chance to say it again. I was wild with hope and despair. You were the one, the only woman I wanted, the only woman who'd ever made me feel I wanted to be with her for the rest of my life, and there was so little of that life left. So much to say and do, and it was too late.

'I wanted for ever with you then, and I want for ever with you now. Marry me. Stay with me always.' He took her in his arms. 'Say yes. Say it quickly.'

'Yes,' she told him joyfully. 'Yes, oh, yes.'

Their kiss was long and deep, an exchange of promises too powerful to need words. Renzo pressed her gently back onto the bed, kissing her face, her neck, moving tenderly down until he came to the flimsy nightdress.

'Why are you so overdressed?' he murmured.

He helped draw it over her head, removed the shorts that were all he wore and pulled her back into his arms as though the urgency that swept through him was too fierce for more delay.

It wasn't the first time they'd made love since their reunion, but this was different. Now they had rediscovered each other in a way that hadn't been true before, and each kiss, each caress, each incitement was imbued with new meaning.

He kissed her breasts softly, teasing,

coaxing until they burned under his touch, making her arch against him in delight. She was demanding and offering in the same moment, clasping her fingers in his hair and pressing her body against his in an urgent plea for more.

'You mean it?' he murmured. 'You'll stay with me always?'

'Always,' she said, speaking with difficulty through her mounting excitement.

'Never leave me.'

'Never…' she vowed, 'never…never…'

Renzo moved over to unite himself with her, knowing that he'd become complete as never before, revelling in that knowledge. He belonged in her bed and her heart, where he would always be welcome.

As he watched her face, soft and tender on the pillow, gazing up at him with trust and love, he understood at last that a new life had begun for him. Now he could claim her with assurance, relying on a love that had already been tested in the fire.

They had first found each other when the future seemed a blank wall. Now it had opened up to bright vistas, gleaming with happiness too long deferred. Further off lay uncertainty, and perhaps beyond that there might be more sadness. But they would be together, and while that was true nothing could ever make them despair.

While they loved, their son slept peacefully in the cot beside them.

They were awoken in the early hours by a knocking on the door and Teresa's voice calling them.

'The hospital called,' she said. 'They think Bruno is dying.'

'Sweet heavens, no!' Renzo exclaimed.

Mandy was already up, dressing Danny, then hurrying down the stairs to where the car was waiting.

On the journey Renzo grasped her hand and sat with his head bent. She knew what he was praying. 'A little longer—just a little longer—'

The nurse was waiting for them, holding open the door.

'He's still alive, but only just.'

Bruno lay on the bed, his eyes closed, his breathing faint. Renzo leaned down and kissed his cheek.

'I'm here, Nonno,' he said, seating himself beside the bed while Mandy sat beside him, with Danny in her arms.

'What do you mean by giving everyone a scare?' Renzo asked in a rallying tone. 'It's nonsense to say that you're dying. You're going to get better, and then we'll have a wonderful time, all of us. We're all here to see you.'

There was an almost pleading note in his voice and Mandy's heart broke for him. This moment meant so much and he'd missed the chance by a fraction.

'Nonno, please open your eyes,' Renzo begged.

There was no change in his breathing and Bruno's eyes didn't open.

'Nonno, *please*,' Renzo said raggedly.

For a moment they thought that nothing would happen, but then, very slowly, the old man's eyes opened and he managed to turn his head very slightly towards Renzo.

But Danny must still be beyond his sight, Mandy thought, suddenly knowing what she must do. She stood up, holding Danny up high in her arms so that the man on the bed could see him. Renzo understood at once and rose from his chair, moving back to let her get closer, and standing just behind her so that Bruno could see them together.

'You were right, Nonno,' Renzo said. 'It's going to be just as you hoped. Do you understand?'

'Yes.' Bruno's voice was almost inaudible, but he was smiling. 'Thank you,' he whispered. 'Now I…can go.'

Then he closed his eyes.

Mandy moved away to let them be together. Renzo kissed his grandfather once more, but it was all over and Bruno didn't move again.

Renzo sat on the bed for a long time, his head bent.

CHAPTER TWELVE

'WHY now?' Renzo asked desperately.

They were at home. He'd told the sad news of Bruno's death to the household, then retreated to be alone with Mandy.

'He'd lived this long,' Renzo mourned. 'Why did he have to die when the future was looking so happy?'

'I think that may have been why,' Mandy said with a sigh. 'He was worried about you. Then he found that you had something to look forward to. That gave him peace, and he didn't have to worry any more.'

Renzo sighed. 'I know you're right. He as good as told me that when you were out of the room. I just wish we could have gone back and told him that our marriage was settled.'

'So do I, but we didn't really need to.'

'Let's make it soon,' he said suddenly. 'We've

been engaged for two years, and that's more than enough.'

'Engaged for two years,' she said, smiling.

'We've belonged to each other since those first two nights. Haven't we?'

'Yes, we have,' she said, reaching for him.

Sue, coming into the room five minutes later, backed hurriedly out without being seen.

She was staying for the wedding, helping the bridal preparations and taking care of Danny while Mandy put in some work for Ferrini. Her new employer had shown a large-minded willingness to take a back seat, and Mandy rewarded him by discovering a new line of enquiry that sent his spirits soaring.

To help her research, Renzo had provided her with a desk in his office, complete with high-powered computer and top-speed broadband. This led to Danny's first visit to the office, where he was welcomed by Lucia and her assistant.

Mandy relinquished him to their care with an easy mind, and Danny had no objection to being treated as a celebrity.

'What are they doing now?' Renzo murmured.

'Lucia is explaining about the Internet,' Mandy replied. 'It's all new to him. I hadn't got around to that yet.'

'But he's only fifteen months old. At that age all I cared about was eating.'

'They didn't have the Internet in those days. It's a new dawn, Renzo, but don't worry. Danny will explain it to you.'

He grinned. 'Kind of him.'

'Lucia,' Mandy said suddenly, 'don't let him climb on the desk.'

But Danny had wriggled out of Lucia's arms and mounted the desk with a little crow of triumph, flailing his arms madly at the machines. Lucia reached for him but she was too late by a split second. The next moment there was a noise that shook the building as the state-of-the-art computer crashed to the floor.

For a moment everyone froze, picturing the mayhem that must have occurred within the shell. Then Danny let out a wail and tried to struggle free of Lucia's protective arms. Mandy hastened towards him, but Renzo fore-stalled her.

'Give him to me,' he said, lifting Danny clear. 'He's just alarmed by the noise. He'll be all right when he's away from it.'

He walked out into the courtyard and settled on a bench in the sun. Mandy, following quickly, heard him talking earnestly in Italian.

'It's nothing to fear—I'm holding you.'

'He's nervous of loud noises,' Mandy told him. 'Ever since a boiler exploded in our building.'

'I don't care for explosions myself,' Renzo observed. To Danny he said, 'But noise is just noise. It can't hurt you. Here—'

He offered his hand and Danny grasped it. His eyes were fixed on his father's face and he was growing calmer.

'You see?' Renzo said. 'We just hold on to each other.'

'Pesce,' Danny replied.

'Sí. Signor Pesce is here.'

Danny grunted.

Mandy backed away, knowing that she wasn't needed here. Returning to the office, she found Lucia frantic.

'It was a new machine,' she wailed. 'It's smashed inside. Is he very angry?'

'He's not angry at all,' Mandy said.

'He must be,' Lucia protested. 'He gets so upset if anything goes wrong. You don't know what he's like.'

'Oh, yes, I do,' Mandy said softly.

'Heavens, he's coming.' Lucia was scrabbling around on the floor.

'Leave it,' Renzo said from the window. 'I doubt it can be repaired. I'm sure you've backed everything up. If not, we'll just have to do it again.'

'But it's brand-new,' Lucia said in a cautious voice, as though suspecting that this was an impostor with Renzo's face. 'Everything up to date—it cost a fortune.'

Renzo shrugged. 'Get onto the insurance.' He gave a wry grimace at his son. 'I'm going to seem like a fool when I tell them who did it, aren't I?'

Danny looked up at him, and suddenly Mandy gave a choke of laughter.

'I could swear he nodded,' she said.

'Of course he did,' Renzo said proudly. 'My son's going to have *bella figura*. You can always tell. Now, let's get him out of here before he puts me out of business.'

Mandy followed him out, just glancing back for a moment to relish the astonished look on Lucia's face.

In the hall courtyard they found Sue, dressed to go out on a joint shopping expedition.

'Are we taking Danny with us?' she asked.

'What do you want to do?' Renzo asked Danny. 'Go trailing round shops or stay here with me?'

'*Pesce,*' Danny declared.

'You've had your answer, ladies. Have fun.' They did have fun, so much so that they stayed out longer than they meant to and got caught in a traffic jam on the way home, arriving late. Renzo greeted them cordially but there was a edginess in his manner that puzzled Mandy. It was a fleeting reminder of the tense, uneasy man he'd been when she'd first arrived.

When Sue had gone upstairs she asked, 'Is something wrong?'

'No,' he said in a slightly forced way.

'Tell me.'

He gave an unconvincing shrug, and tried to speak lightly. 'I thought you'd be here hours ago. I looked for you—'

Going through room after room, finding them all empty.

Mandy groaned silently as she understood how she'd accidentally roused his demons.

'I'm sorry, I should have called. Why didn't you call me? I had my phone.'

'I didn't want you to feel that I was tracking your every movement, being suffocatingly possessive.' He gave a slightly strained laugh. 'Not until I've got you safely married. Then you might get a shock at how possessive I am.'

'But, since I belong to you completely, what is there to be possessive about?' she asked tenderly. 'Oh, you dear fool.'

'Yes, I'm a fool. I knew you were coming

home; it's just that—' he gave a self-mocking shrug '—I don't like it when you're not there. Neither does Danny.'

'I knew he'd be all right with you.'

'But you're the one he wants, and the one I want. He and I are agreed on that.'

She kissed him. 'I'm going to have to be careful if my menfolk are in such perfect accord. In no time at all you'll be ganging up on me.'

Renzo nodded. 'You'd better believe it.'

He led her into the living room and closed the door.

'I need to tell you something,' he said. 'I've read Nonno's will and it came as a shock. He's left every penny to me, not to my mother.'

'Teresa told me he was angry with her for leaving you.'

'Even so, she has three other children who should be considered. I don't think I can accept all of it. I thought I'd take his share of the business, and some of the money for Danny. Nonno would have wanted that. The rest can be divided between her and her children.'

'That sounds like a good idea.'

'You agree?'

'But it has nothing to do with me.'

'If you're going to be my wife, it has everything to do with you. I'm giving away money that I could have spent on you, decking you with diamonds.'

'I don't like diamonds. Too cold. Let them have it.'

'Wait till you hear how much it is before you give it away.'

He told her the figure.

'How much?'

'I knew he was rich, but not that rich,' Renzo said. 'Do you want to change your mind?'

'No, I still think your idea is best.'

'So I have your permission?' he asked with an air of submissiveness that made her lips twitch.

'I'll thump you one in a minute,' she threatened.

'Nothing changes. Those were almost the first words you spoke to me.'

'And they'll probably be the last,' she predicted. 'Fifty years on, I'll still be trying to keep you in line, still with no success.'

'I don't like the idea of fifty years,' he said.

'Too much?'

'Too little. I want at least seventy.'

'And you'll probably get your way, then as always.'

After a moment she asked cautiously, 'What about your mother? Will she come over for her father's funeral, or our wedding?'

'I don't know.'

'Have you spoken to her?'

'I called her in Australia to tell her of his death, and then again yesterday to give her the date of the funeral. Both times I found myself talking to her husband. He promised to pass the messages on, but I've heard nothing. Now I've agreed matters with you I'll call the lawyer and tell him what we've decided. Then he can let her know.'

The lawyer arrived without warning the next day.

'I've had your mother on the phone, demanding to know how much she'd inherited,' he said distractedly.

'How did she react when you told her?' Renzo asked wryly.

'Blasted my ear off.' He rubbed his ear as though he could still hear the shrill rant. 'I told her how you were going to share out the money and she just screamed louder. She says it's hers by right and she wants it all.

'I explained that if she challenged the will it would cause delays. She called you a few choice names, then slammed the phone down. I don't think she'll give any more trouble.'

'Fine, I'll leave it all to you,' Renzo said. 'Then please draw up the paperwork putting Danny's share in trust until he's older.'

'With yourself as the trustee, presumably?'

'Jointly with his mother,' Renzo said.

When they were alone he glanced up at Mandy.

'All I feel is pity for her,' he said. 'She could have met Danny, her first grandchild. If she'd loved Nonno, she'd have been happy to see that Danny is so much like him.

'As it is, she's missing so much happiness and she'll never know. Let her go. And don't worry about me. She has no power over me of any kind.' He dropped his voice to add quietly, 'Only one person has that power, and she may use it as she likes.'

Bruno's funeral took place three days later in a church packed with everyone who had known him and loved him in earlier days. The only notable exception was his daughter, who neither came nor sent a message.

The wedding was scheduled for two days later. Ferrini, who had friends in high places, pulled strings to get it scheduled so fast. Teresa had hysterics at the thought of devising a wedding feast so soon after cooking the funeral meats, but was clearly enjoying the challenge.

'She's very superstitious about us seeing each other before the wedding tomorrow,' Renzo told Mandy that night as they stood at the window, looking at the moon.

'She'd be even more superstitious if she could see you here in my room,' she said.

'Shall I go? I only want to do what's right.'

'You don't mean a word of that,' she said indignantly. 'You're just trying to wind me up.'

'I can't fool you, can I?'

'You'd better believe it. Are you sure you aren't having second thoughts? Does any man really want a wife who knows him that well?'

Renzo's fingertips briefly lingered on her face. 'He does if he has any sense.'

'Be warned. I'm a lioness with sharp claws.'

'Not a lioness,' he said softly. 'A little cat.'

There was a joyful contentment in his voice, and her heart lifted.

'Beware,' she teased. 'I'll lead you a merry dance.'

'I'm sure of it. I might lead you one.'

'That's something that's not going to change. You always were the most infuriating man I'd ever met, and you always will be.' She brightened. 'But at least you'll never be boring.'

'We'll fight,' he agreed with satisfaction. 'And I'll let you win, like I always did.'

'Let me— You cheeky—'

'Why don't we stop wasting time?' he said, taking her into his arms.

* * *

It was going to be a simple wedding. The bride, wearing a dress of ivory satin, would travel to the church accompanied by her bridesmaid, Sue, and Danny. An old friend of Renzo's was to give the bride away, and Ferrini would be the best man.

Teresa was still worrying because the bride and groom were together before the wedding. 'It's bad luck,' she protested.

But Renzo resisted her attempts to make him hide in another room.

'We've already had all our bad luck,' he said. 'No misfortune can befall us now.'

As he said it he gave Mandy a smile that reached across great distances of space and time to a world where only they existed. Teresa saw it and was silenced.

'It's time for the groom and me to depart,' Ferrini said, winking at Mandy, who winked back.

'What's going on?' Renzo asked, looking from one to the other.

'He's reassuring me that our little plan is going to work out all right,' Mandy told him.

'What little plan?'

'Wait and see.'

'Do you know about this plan?' Renzo asked Sue, receiving a nod in return. 'But you're not going to tell me, are you?'

'She threatened me with dire retribution if I did,' Sue said mischievously.

With that he had to be content.

As he left for the church Mandy watched him until the last minute. Then it was time for the next car, with all the staff. Finally the best man handed her and Sue into the car, and they made the journey to the church with Danny sitting on Sue's lap.

As she headed down the aisle she saw Renzo standing before the altar. He was looking back in her direction, relaxing when he could see her.

As she came close, he reached out to her, taking her hand in his own, smiling into her eyes. The priest appeared and the wedding began.

Everything proceeded without a hitch until they came to the exchange of rings.

This was the moment when the plan that she, Sue and Ferrini had hatched together should be put into effect. Ferrini should have handed the rings to Renzo. Instead, he put them into Danny's plump little hand and stood back to let Sue, holding Danny, move closer to Renzo.

He smiled, understanding, and reached to take the rings from his son. But Danny had his own ideas and refused to let them go. When Renzo tried to ease them away, he found a finger poked into his eye.

'Ow,' he said softly, rubbing the affected part.

'He didn't mean it,' Mandy said quickly.

'Leave it to us,' Renzo told her. 'This is between men.'

He confronted his son, who confronted him back.

'So it's going to be like that, is it?' he asked and, to Mandy's delight, a broad smile spread across his face. 'You're going to be trouble, aren't you?'

Danny nodded.

'Good for you,' Renzo said. 'Now, can I have them, please?'

Danny considered, then handed them over, at the same time sticking out his tongue defiantly. Renzo promptly returned the compliment.

The priest coughed.

'Sorry, Father,' Renzo said self-consciously.

Mandy smiled with relief that the little plan had worked better than she'd dared to hope. But now she found that Renzo, in his turn, had a surprise for her. As he slid the ring onto her finger he spoke words that had never been said in any marriage service before.

'Take this ring, whose circle is a symbol of never ending love. Our love began with the approach of death, but it lived, as it will always live, and will last for ever. I belonged to you then, I belong to you now. I will always belong to you.'

She had to pause for a moment to choke back her tears, before managing to say, 'I have belonged to you from the first moment, though it took me a little time to understand it. But, when I did understand, I knew that there was no going back.' She paused for a moment before repeating to him the words he'd spoken to her in what might have been their last hours. 'You are everything to me, and you will be everything, for however long we have—and afterwards.'

He nodded, showing that he remembered. Then he kissed her before the whole congregation.

She recalled little about the rest of the service. She only knew that now she was his wife, a part of him as he was part of her, as fate had always meant her to be.

By the time they left the church the solemn mood had lightened. Looking at the photographs afterwards, she saw Renzo and herself, alight with triumph at having 'held hands and jumped' together. His smile was the one she'd seen two years earlier and hadn't dared hope ever to see again.

The best picture of all showed Renzo with his son in his arms, the two of them exchanging knowing grins.

At the reception everybody toasted everybody, accompanied by witty speeches. Teresa was toasted for producing a splendid meal. Sue was toasted, thanked and wished a pleasant journey for the next day.

But for the most important toast of all there was no speech, when Renzo silently raised his glass to his bride, unnoticed by anyone except themselves.

It seemed an age until they could be alone together, but at last everyone had gone and they lay in each other's arms.

'You were wonderful with Danny,' she said, marvelling. 'When I think how I used to worry about you two.'

'No need. I knew we were going to be all right that night when I sat by his cot. And I knew it again today when he put his tongue out. Nonno and I used to play that game when I was a child, and suddenly there I was, playing it again. We just needed time to find each other.'

'It's just a pity about your mother.'

'Forget her. She doesn't matter any more. Only you and Danny matter. There was a time when even the thought of her was painful, as though a bleak, empty place had opened up inside me.'

His voice was suddenly filled with wonder. 'But now it's all gone, the darkness, the empti-ness. I look into what used to be a void and I see only you—the one I love, the one I will always love.'

He took her tenderly into his arms.

'And where you are,' he whispered, 'there can never be darkness.'

MILLS & BOON
Romance

On sale 5th June 2009

Travel to tropical shores with the start of our brand new mini-series Escape Around the World *and don't miss the final instalment in the* www.blinddatebrides.com *trilogy!*

OUTBACK HEIRESS, SURPRISE PROPOSAL
by Margaret Way

After inheriting half of her grandfather's empire, Francesca must fight the re-ignition of old flames when she discovers the joint heir is her childhood sweetheart Bryn…

HONEYMOON WITH THE BOSS *by Jessica Hart*

Escape to the sandy shores of the Indian Ocean when Imogen's boss's marriage of convenience falls through and the honeymoon becomes a tropical business trip!

HIS PRINCESS IN THE MAKING *by Melissa James*

Toby has always secretly loved his best friend Lia. But when Lia discovers she's *Suddenly Royal!* and a princess, Toby must compete with an entire kingdom for her attention!

DREAM DATE WITH THE MILLIONAIRE
by Melissa McClone

When *www.blinddatebrides.com* pairs her with gorgeous millionaire Bryce, bombshell Dani thinks he will judge her poor background like every man does…but Bryce isn't just any man!

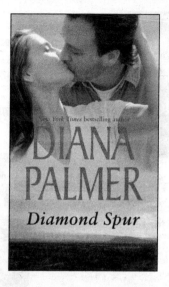

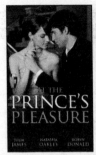

FREE

2 BOOKS AND A SURPRISE GIFT!

We would like to take this opportunity to thank you for reading this Mills & Boon® book by offering you the chance to take TWO more specially selected titles from the Romance series absolutely FREE! We're also making this offer to introduce you to the benefits of the Mills & Boon® Book Club™ —

- ★ **FREE home delivery**
- ★ **FREE gifts and competitions**
- ★ **FREE monthly Newsletter**
- ★ **Books available before they're in the shops**
- ★ **Exclusive Mills & Boon Book Club offers**

Accepting these FREE books and gift places you under no obligation to buy; you may cancel at any time, even after receiving your free shipment. Simply complete your details below and return the entire page to the address below. You don't even need a stamp!

YES! Please send me 2 free Romance books and a surprise gift. I understand that unless you hear from me, I will receive 4 superb new titles every month for just £2.99 each, postage and packing free. I am under no obligation to purchase any books and may cancel my subscription at any time. The free books and gift will be mine to keep in any case.

N9ZEE

Ms/Mrs/Miss/Mr...Initials ....
                                                                                                   BLOCK CAPITALS PLEASE

Surname ....

Address ....

....

....Postcode ....

Send this whole page to:
The Mills & Boon Book Club, FREEPOST CN81, Croydon, CR9 3WZ